I Haven't Dreamed of
Flying for a While

I Haven't Dreamed of Flying for a While

Taichi Yamada

Translated by David James Karashima

faber and faber

First published in the UK in 2008
by Faber and Faber Limited
3 Queen Square London WC1N 3AU

Originally published in Japan as *Tobu Yume Wo Shibaraku Minai*
by Shinchosha Co. Ltd, Tokyo, in 1989
British edition rights arranged by Taichi Yamada
through The Marsh Agency Ltd/Japan Foreign Rights Centre

Typeset by Faber and Faber Ltd
Printed in England by Mackays of Chatham, plc

A CIP record for this book
is available from the British Library

ISBN 978-0-571-23497-4

2 4 6 8 10 9 7 5 3 1

I talked about how I hadn't dreamed of flying for a while,
And that very night, for the first time in a while,
I dreamt I was flying.

From 'Dream' by Sachiko Yoshihara

Prologue

It started in winter, just two and a half months before my forty-eighth birthday. There I was, confined to my hospital bed with a fractured thigh, when suddenly I realised I was becoming detached from this world.

Please forgive my rather pretentious beginning. It's just that the story I'm about to tell is of a unique experience. It's also one that I still can't make up my mind about – not even now it's a thing of the past.

On any day I can come up with several different explanations for what happened, only to shoot them all down immediately. On some days, I cling desperately to one particular answer; then on others, I give up trying to make sense of it altogether.

Let me start by telling you some of the things I consider to be part of this world.

There are the many elements of my life as deputy sales director of the Northern Japan branch of a prefab construction company. These include living away from my family, management responsibility, sales performance, the booming tradesman's voice of our branch president, my department director's shameless instinct for self-preservation, the interest rate of the Government Housing Loan Corporation, the feigned enthusiasm of my junior staff, a wife in Tokyo, a daughter who married and left home, a son in his second year of university (and the unfortunate way things are between us), nervous insomnia, gastrointestinal neurosis, an over-frequent need to urinate and many other aspects too numerous to mention.

I never would have thought I could become detached from all these things after just ten or so bedridden days. But when you spend most of your time staring up at a white ceiling, you can soon start to feel like you're floating further and further away. Or perhaps I'd just given up.

Despite my reluctance to admit it, the feeling that my career had come to a dead end had soaked through me like water into a cotton rag, right from the very moment I got injured. And though this sense seemed to press down on me with a great weight, it was probably the great mass of the sensation that actually helped me unload it, allowing a new me to surface; one that until now had been pushed deep down inside.

Okay, it might seem a little over the top for me to put it that way. But one morning I just suddenly felt as free as an adolescent. I was overwhelmed at my newfound freedom, by how long it had been since I'd felt that way and by how much I'd been repressing. And then there was the premonition. At least, that's what I think it was. After all, I'd never experienced one before and the whole thing was completely alien to me. I'd certainly never predicted the future before.

I had been working in a company that relied entirely on official data and left no room whatsoever for personal instinct. It was an environment that suited me well as someone who'd never relied on intuition, not even in my personal life. So when the premonition came to me, I didn't even recognise it.

It arrived out of the blue early one afternoon.

I was nodding off when it hit me like the crack of a whip.

First, I felt it in my stomach. Then a surge of suffocating anxiety welled up around my chest, forcing me to open my eyes. Before I knew it, a sense of urgency had overwhelmed my entire body, impelling me to open my mouth. My immediate impulse was to try not to let out a cry. So instead, I concentrated on taking deep breaths to repress the mounting sense of restlessness.

It had to be a dream. I had to have been dreaming. But it certainly hadn't felt like a dream. My entire body was seething with an unfathomable sense of immediacy and my heart was pounding. The term 'cardioneurosis' crossed my mind and I tried with all my willpower to suppress this sudden attack.

I noticed the soft light shining onto the white ceiling and the wilting red carnation standing still in its vase. Everything else around me was motionless too – but then, I hadn't felt myself moving either. The leg that was fixed in place hadn't budged and I thought maybe there was something wrong with me – to make me lose my breath, break out into a sweat and be clutching my blanket over nothing.

'Calm down,' I told myself, 'It's nothing.'

Then I heard the voices of children outside. And the laughter of the young nurse, Ms Nakanobu. The sound of a car boot being shut – probably somebody being discharged from the hospital – reminding me that I should check with someone on the appropriate amount to leave the nurses to show my gratitude. There must be a standard amount for patients in private rooms, I thought, but there were no other hospitals in this area. And for all I knew, that sort of thing might not even be expected at this one. On the other hand, it might be an even bigger deal out here in the countryside.

Then, as I was immersed in these thoughts, I was struck by

another wave of urgency and I held my breath to try to keep it at bay.

That's when I heard a train far away in the distance.

A withering sensation rushed through me. A strong shiver spreading from the pit of my stomach to my chest. Then it all became clear. I could see it vividly. The train derailing and rolling over. But why was I thinking that? Feeling that? Was I losing my mind?

All those feelings of urgency and restlessness had nowhere to go until that point. But now they focused themselves on the sound of the train speeding along the tracks. But there was nothing out of the ordinary about that sound. The only thing out of the ordinary was me. I listened to the sound, searching for even a hint that something was wrong. But there was nothing like that at all. Just the sound of the train coming closer and closer, like every other train I've heard on the Hokuriku Line since I'd been in here.

But my heart continued to beat faster. The train continued to come closer. And I covered my mouth with the back of my hand – afraid of letting out a cry. What was happening to me? Why were my nerves torturing me? Fear overwhelmed me.

'Stop!' I shouted, 'Stop!'

Then I shoved my fist in my mouth to stifle myself, while the engine maintained its speed, its velocity and its pounding, timely rhythm.

There was nothing I could do.

Nothing.

I covered my face.

The roar boomed on.

Moving forward.

Getting louder.
Building power.
And then . . . a split-second of silence.
The ground began to rumble.
Metal thrashed and tumbled.
And my story. It began.

1

The noise of the helicopter above drowned out the sound of the TV as it flew over the hospital, then across the fuzzy TV screen, before providing a bird's-eye view of the devastation below. Two train carriages lay overturned and a third was derailed but upright. The remaining seven carriages were still on the tracks. Fourteen people were dead and more than sixty were injured and the Hokuriku Line express train *Snow Grouse* accident went on being reported throughout the day.

Although the accident had happened so close by, I couldn't even look out of the window to see what was going on. Although the television was my only source of information, it at least gave me the opportunity to see the outside of the building into which I'd been carried ten days earlier – even from the sky. It was built along a national highway that ran parallel to the railway tracks, and all that surrounded the hospital, other than a few houses here and there, were snow-covered fields.

According to the news, thirty-one of the injured had been brought to this hospital from the crash site and tents had been set up by the main entrance as a makeshift emergency centre. I saw a reporter reading out the names of the dead on TV. And behind the reporter, I could see the window of what was probably my room.

After the NHK broadcast ended, I flipped through the other TV channels, turning down the volume whenever commercials came on. Then I heard the sound of someone running down the hall in slippers followed by a flurry of excited voices that filled the fifth floor.

'Don't use the lift!' 'It's terrible.' 'Get to the second-floor hall-way.'

The noise of ambulances and human cries continued almost ceaselessly throughout the first several hours of the afternoon. And mixed in among them was the leisurely voice of someone guiding a driver in the parking lot.

'Okay, okay, a little to the right. All right, all right.'

So calm, so ordinary, it was a voice that made me feel that what was going on outside was not the same as this tragedy unfolding on my screen.

Lunch was served at three.

'Sorry it's late,' said the lady in her fifties who brought it. She was uncharacteristically quiet and didn't smile as much as usual either.

'How is it?'

'Huh?'

'Is it really bad down there?'

'Hmm.'

I'd touched a nerve. She crouched down without answering and turned the bed handle. As the back of my bed rose, I observed her expression. She looked annoyed, which surprised me a little since she was usually so playful. It was possible that she was just in a foul mood and that it had nothing to do with the accident. But for the first time I actually felt I'd experienced the accident at first hand – a shocking event that had occurred so close by, yet which I could witness only by television. I imagined the horror of the lower levels of the hospital and the scenes that had silenced this usually chatty woman.

'Enjoy,' she said, and the door shut abruptly. I felt her annoyance at me, even though I'd done nothing wrong.

Since the accident, I'd thought about the premonition many times and I eventually decided it was probably a kind of illusion. Like the way people who fall out of bed (although you don't hear of that happening so much these days) can have a long dream with a plot leading up to the fall, I'd probably been asleep until the accident had happened. Then I'd dreamed about a premonition in the split-second between hearing the accident and waking up. Although that split-second had felt like five minutes or more in my dream. It was an implausible explanation, but it seemed no more improbable than the chances of someone like me, who had nothing to do with the accident, having a premonition about it. In this way, I convinced myself it was nothing more than a dream by the end of the afternoon.

A little later, just before six o'clock, the head nurse came into my room with a young nurse named Ms Ozaki.

'What should we do?' she said with the professionalism of someone immersed in their duties.

'What on earth should we do about it?' she said again, looking at me as if I were a piece of furniture.

'About what?' I asked.

'Oh.' She laughed, as if she'd only just noticed me. 'I'm sorry.'

Then she quickly straightened out the duvet around my shoulder, turned to the young nurse and asked her, 'Do you think it would upset him?'

She turned and looked down at me again.

'What should I do?' she said.

'About what?' I asked again.

'If you're really against it, we can put another bed in the six-person room. But as you can guess, we're having difficulty with room arrangements.'

'I see.'

'It wouldn't have been so bad if we weren't already fully occupied. But even in normal circumstances, twenty is the maximum number of emergency patients we're equipped to handle. Right now, we have thirty, some of whom are on mattresses on the floor.'

'And what do you want me to do?'

'Well, the director is saying he will do something about it by tomorrow morning. But would you mind moving to the single room on the other end of this floor for now?'

'Not at all.'

'Good, but the thing is, though I say it's a single room, it's actually already occupied. So there'll be two of you in one small room. The other person has already said it would be okay. And we would also put a partition up. So what do you think?'

'The other person doesn't have anything contagious, right?'

'No. Similar to you. Bruising and fractures. Can't move either, but nothing serious.'

'Then there isn't even a need for a partition. I'll move.'

'Actually the partition was requested by the other patient. It's a woman, you see.'

' . . . Ah.'

'But, as I say, neither of you is able to move and it is just for the one night.'

'Well, I guess there's nothing more for me to say. It's up to the other patient, then,' I said with a blank expression and in a matter-of-fact tone.

Neither the head nurse nor Ms Ozaki showed any sign of understanding how it would make a middle-aged man feel to be asked to share a room with a woman. The head nurse simply said, 'That's a relief,' and the next thing I knew I was placed on a rolling bed and pushed out into the hallway.

Throughout this time, I noticed the head nurse hadn't said anything that might hint at the age of the woman, and I got the feeling that she was doing so deliberately. Could the fact that she'd asked for a partition mean that it was a young woman? No, surely they wouldn't put a young woman in the same room with a man, even if the man weren't able to move. She'd be the same age as myself at the youngest. Or much older. That was more likely. The nurses were probably pretending to act indifferent and getting a kick out of thinking of all the things I was imagining. But then again, surely the nurses wouldn't have the time for such things, given the current situation. Had they simply said nothing because it wasn't even worth mentioning? Or did the fact that I was thinking about it so much simply mean I had a dirty mind? Either way, I was starting to feel irritated that all of these thoughts were occupying my mind.

As I was transferred from the eastern end of the floor to the corner room on the western end I worried a little about what the other patients, in their boredom, would make of my move. But it turned out that there wasn't anyone in the hallway to see. Then I realised that the other patients were probably anything *but* bored on this particular day, before turning my thoughts to the evening news, which would have already started.

'Sorry to bother you again,' said the head nurse as she opened the door of room 513.

'It's okay,' came a quiet response.

It sounded like a woman in her forties. Or perhaps in her thirties? I replayed the voice in my head as I was carted into the room, but I came to no clear decision. The first thing that came into sight was the partition. A steel pipe frame holding up a light blue cloth. It wasn't very tall, but it was wide enough so that I could only see the very end of the other bed.

'This is Mr Taura. The man I mentioned,' said the head nurse to the woman.

'This is Ms Miyabayashi,' said the nurse, looking at me.

'Hello,' I said to the blue piece of cloth.

'Hello. Nice to meet you.'

Her voice was frail. I got the impression that it had taken a great deal of effort to squeeze out those words.

'Since neither of you can move from your beds, we've asked you a favour we wouldn't normally ask. But this is an emergency arrangement, and as soon as we're able to move even some of the people from today, we will have everything back to normal. So please accept our apologies for the inconvenience.'

After that, the two of us were left alone.

The woman was breathlessly silent. Not fifteen minutes had passed since the head nurse had walked into my original room and I was already wondering if I'd agreed to all this a bit hastily. The two beds were closer than I had expected and although the partition just about separated our two sides, it suddenly struck me just how odd an arrangement this was. I also noticed that the partition was blocking my view of the window. As for the television, it was on the shelf above and to the left of the door, where it was most likely out of the woman's sight. I could watch it, but I had to turn my neck and look up to manage it. The woman's bed that had been facing the window had been moved to the side and the room was barely large enough to fit in the partition and my additional makeshift bed. Had there really been no other option?

Even taking the emergency into account, I found it hard to believe that they had to resort to such an arrangement. I briefly wondered if they were playing some kind of joke on us, but surely they wouldn't do that on a day like this. Then there was the issue of the woman's age. She may not have been really young, but I was still surprised the nurses didn't worry about a middle-aged man turning lustful. I regretted having agreed to put myself in such a situation, but I couldn't tell them to take me back now.

The woman let out a sigh, which gave me quite a start. It felt close and it sounded as if she'd been holding her breath as I'd suspected. But it sounded soft. I turned my face away, not wanting to react. I wanted to be left alone. Though of course the woman *was* leaving me alone. All she'd done was let out a breath and I felt bad for reacting with such hostility, though I think it was more a case of me trying to put a lid on my feelings. I knew the reason, too. It was because of my wife.

I would hasten to add that my wife hadn't actually done anything wrong. But I was reminded of the telegram she'd sent me the morning after I'd fractured my leg.

SHOCKED TO LEARN OF YOUR SERIOUS INJURY. THOUGHT I SHOULD GO OVER STRAIGHT AWAY BUT MR ENAMI GAVE ME YOUR MESSAGE ON THE PHONE NOT TO GO TO THE TROUBLE SO I WILL ACCEPT YOUR KIND OFFER SINCE DEADLINE FOR FEB ISSUE IS NEAR. SORRY. PLEASE TAKE CARE. TOSHIE.

She was editing a town magazine with two other people and I believe she'd made the right decision. I was glad she hadn't come.

It was only a fractured thighbone, after all, and although I couldn't move from the bed since I'd fractured the only bone in the thigh, there was no chance of any complication. I was told that the surrounding muscle had hardly been damaged. It was swollen and there was pain and fever, but these were things I would simply have to live with for a while.

'That worked out for the best, thank you,' I'd said to Enami, the assistant manager. 'I mean, there's nothing she could do if she did come. All you can do when you have a fracture is lie in bed. There's no reason for her to sacrifice her work and fly all the way over just for appearances.'

'You're very understanding,' said Enami, but I could tell from the tone of his voice that he pitied me. True, if you looked at my situation as a whole, I could understand why people might feel sorry for me. But as far as my wife was concerned, it really was better if she didn't come. It was simply much easier for me to relax without her around.

My wife had come to understand what work was all about. She used to criticise me by saying, 'You think you can get away with anything if you say it's for your job.' So when she'd told me that she couldn't come because of her work, it gave me a feeling of satisfaction – like I'd gotten back at her somehow.

In the spring four years ago, soon after my nineteen-year-old daughter had announced that she was getting married, my wife had begun to lose her senses. She'd cry that she'd used up her life for our two children and me. She threw things at me. She started seeing a doctor, who gave her medicine that made her lethargic, and that made her sleep all day. Soon after that, my daughter married a twenty-six-year-old guy working at a light electric appliances company and left home. Then my wife began working for a town magazine as an unpaid volunteer, which helped her regain her spirits. Half a year later, she quit that magazine and started a similar monthly magazine that operated on advertisement revenue. She hired two women, and although things seemed difficult for the first year, it was now doing much better than the other town magazine. She even appeared to be making about 2–300,000 yen a month.

Having such an ability, yet dedicating her life to taking care of her family, it was no surprise that she'd gone a little crazy. So when I was told of my move to the Northern Japan branch office a year ago, I told my wife that I would go alone. If I hadn't suggested it first, she might have done so herself. But I had no intention of making my wife quit her work. My son had just started at university as well, so it only made sense that I went alone.

'I hear it can get really lonely,' said my wife, despite clearly having no intention of coming with me.

'It'll be nothing,' I said.

I didn't want to risk her going back to being a worn-out, nagging wife. I didn't want to feel that I owed her, either.

Every so often I would feel small flashes of animosity and I can't say for sure whether they were directed towards my wife. For example, I felt animosity about the brusque way the nurses snatched the thermometer when I handed it to them. When I heard a young woman visitor in the corridor say, 'Well, take care, then,' I was repulsed by her accent and annoyed at her lack of sincerity. And even when a young lady from work brought me carnations, I resented her awkward manner of speaking, her insensitivity and her hideous but healthy features.

For several days, my hours were dominated by uncontrollable feelings of hatred with which I didn't know what to do. But owing to the way my hatred was always directed at women, I felt such feelings stemmed from my relationship with my wife. Maybe somewhere inside I'd wished my wife were the type to drop everything and rush over as soon as she'd learned I'd been injured.

But then again, who was I to feel this way? I was a man who had always put work first. I'd never considered taking time off when my wife had a fever and our children were still young, so I couldn't criticise my wife for prioritising her job. She, like any human being, had an ego. She had the right to utilise it too, and to maximise its potential. My wishes were purely selfish. And my wishes were impossible. My wife wasn't worried about her injured husband. She didn't even want to see him.

This made the egos of women in general look enlarged to me. It made me feel that, though they may put on a friendly face, they were in fact all egomaniacs who would never devote their hearts to anything other than themselves (though I knew very well that I myself didn't devote my heart to my wife, so such thinking was selfish). I felt determined not to feel sexually attracted to such selfish women and not even to act friendly towards them.

About two or three days later, I became able to see these feelings from a distance and to laugh at myself for my immaturity. I felt my harsh feelings melt away and disappear. And in the end, it was a relief that my wife was concentrating on herself. It was much better than her coming along and being irritable. I might have felt lonelier for it, but it wasn't a feeling I wasn't used to. I was happier for the freedom it gave me and I was enjoying the nostalgic feeling of an adolescent nursing a broken heart.

So at the moment when my new female neighbour sighed, I turned my face away. I was determined not to be stimulated by something like that. Determined not to let my guard down and grab at silk, only to find a sharp metal item hidden underneath. I'd had enough of that kind of thing already. Perhaps this meant that I was still harbouring a grudge against my wife.

Even after night fell, the clanking of metal and the voices of workers restoring the railway reverberated like the sounds of a faraway festival.

'I don't,' I said to the blue sheet, 'want to impose.'

I felt her let out a breath on the other side of the partition, followed by a fragile 'Yes'.

'Being in the same room like this . . . and not saying anything . . . I feel like I'm being inconsiderate.'

'Inconsiderate?' she said in a soft voice.

'I mean, when a man and a woman are in the same room and there is a long silence, it seems to me that is the man's fault. At least that is how I feel somehow.'

I heard her shift her body slightly.

'You could say in a sense that we're in separate wards, but I'm not sure exactly how separate we can say this room is. So, I felt I ought to say something.'

There was a moment's pause, then she said, 'Yes.' Her voice was soft.

'That's all.'

'Yes.'

'They're late with our supper aren't they?'

'Yes.' She paused before continuing, 'Yes, they certainly are late.' I sensed something like a small smile in her words. And just that made me feel so much more at ease. Perhaps it was because of her soft voice. Perhaps it had been because she'd received my words so smoothly.

As it happens, I had actually thought of various other ways of starting the conversation. I could have started with, 'Have you been here long?' I could have sighed and apologised for lying in the bed next to hers by saying, 'What a stroke of bad luck. This must be such an inconvenience to you.' Or I could have started by saying how surprising the accident was.

But the words that came out when I opened my mouth were completely different from what I had expected. They were words that didn't suit the usual me. Deputy sales directors of prefab construction manufacturers didn't speak like that, you see. Besides, you couldn't speak like that around here and expect people to accept it.

But the words that drifted naturally towards the other side of the blue cloth were accepted quietly, which left me with a calm feeling. It was quite possible that it was just my wishful thinking. That she was actually too sick to bother mocking my pretentiousness. I wondered what must be wrong with me to exaggerate the meaning behind just a few words. I just hadn't been myself the past few months.

Finally, I could hear the meal wagon rolling down the hall. Doors were swung open and slammed shut. Actually, they weren't so rough with the doors, but it did seem that way when you were in bed.

'Supper time. Sorry we're late.' It was the voice of Nurse

Muraoka. Had the part-time meal lady who was so down at lunch gone home sick?

The door opened and I felt the hallway breeze drift into the room.

'Supper time. Sorry we're late.'

Suddenly I felt embarrassed, as if I'd been caught hiding with a woman. It was a feeling I hadn't had for a long, long time.

'Not the usual lady today?' I asked, my voice cracking slightly.

'No. Are you disappointed?' she replied without breaking her cheerful gait. 'You know, five or six others have asked me that already. She must be popular.'

'Actually, I mentioned it because I was glad. You're much better.'

'Thank you! I'll make sure to tell her tomorrow.'

'You'd do that? Even though I paid you a compliment? Well, I *was* going to play matchmaker for you, but not any more.'

'Oh that's too bad.'

I laughed heartily, but once she'd left I felt a little embarrassed – like I'd been inconsiderate to the woman on the other side of the partition. She was lying there silent. Perhaps she'd smiled a little, but I couldn't see.

So then we had dinner, just the two of us.

The sounds of tableware. The sounds of eating. The sounds of drinking.

'So you've got some sort of injury?' I said.

'Yes. A lumbar fracture. At least, I think that's what you call it.'

'I see.'

I was about to ask how she had injured herself but decided against it. After all, I couldn't ask how she had injured herself without telling her how I had injured myself. And I didn't want to do that.

'I'm in for my right leg. The thighbone. I have something that looks like a ladder covered in cotton as a splint, and I've been confined to bed for ten days already.'

'I see . . .' she whispered.

I got the sense that she didn't want to talk, so I stopped talking.

The sounds of tableware began again. The sounds of eating. Of drinking.

Just after nine, a nurse came in and turned on the television.

'Mr Taura, please watch this for a moment, would you?' said the elderly nurse as laughter poured out of the TV set above me.

'Why?'

'Just because,' said the nurse, and returned to the woman's side.

Perplexed, I looked up at the TV as told. It was a quiz show. If I'd wanted to watch something, I'd have wanted to watch news footage of the crash. They might be showing images from the scene as the wreckage removal went on through the night. It was probably the top news of the day. But then again, even if I turned to NHK at thirteen minutes past nine, news of the crash would probably be over by then.

Then I noticed a faint smell of urine.

I was also using a urine bottle. Did this mean I was supposed to turn on the TV before using it? What if I wanted to use it in the middle of the night?

Even after ten, I could hear people working in the distance.

The woman murmured something. Or at least I thought she did.

'Pardon?'

But there was no answer. The light was already off. Perhaps she was talking in her sleep.

Sleep talking. That's something I was afraid I would do. That's why I'd been so adamant to the colleague who signed me into the hospital that I wanted a private room. Who knows what I could be saying in my sleep! I might even cry and I wouldn't want anyone else to hear that. In the end, I was more afraid that I wouldn't sleep well because of my fear of what might happen if I did. I had difficulty sleeping as it was and I didn't want to add to my worries.

'I'm a little embarrassed,' said the woman. I turned to face her direction, quite sure that she wasn't talking in her sleep.

'Pardon?'

'I sometimes talk to myself. I've been in a private room all this time. So I haven't had to be careful. That's why I just spoke out loud without thinking about it.'

'I didn't really hear anything.'

'Well, you said "Pardon?"'

'I couldn't make out what you said.'

'Okay.'

'I do the same, you know. Talk to myself. Exactly the same thing. If I'm not thinking, I forget I'm not alone and I say things out loud too.'

'I'll try not to listen.'

'Let's both do that.'

Silence again. In the distance, I could hear the sound of a large piece of metal being moved. I still had the impression that she was either in her thirties or in her early forties and I wondered which it was. Her soft, delicate voice made me imagine a small, thin woman. I was accustomed to disappointment and so I stopped myself from guessing whether she would be beautiful or not.

'In this *shishuu* . . .' she started.

Did she mean *shishuu* as in embroidery? As in collection of poems? As in the stench of death?

'Yes?' I replied.

'Well, I was wondering if you'd mind if–'

'No. I'm listening. Don't worry, I don't think I'll be able to fall asleep early tonight.

'I mean because of the accident; it's got my heart beating faster and my mind wide awake,' I added quickly, afraid she might think I couldn't sleep because a woman was lying next to me.

'Well, in this poem . . .'

'Poem?'

'Yes. Poem. *Shishuu* as in collection of poems. Is my pronunciation strange?'

'Not at all. I just thought you meant *shishuu* as in embroidery.'

'Is there a difference?'

'How do you mean?'

'In the pronunciation between the two.'

'No, it's probably the same.'

'I'm from Yokohama, maybe that's it.'

'Do you live there?'

'No. I was born there.'

'Of course. You couldn't be living there.'

'But you're from Tokyo, aren't you?'

'Yes, but it's unusual for a woman to be in my situation.'

'It's been a long time . . .'

'Pardon?'

'A long time here . . .'

'Oh.'

'I've picked up the accent.'

'But I think that's nice. To have a slight accent . . .'

Having grown up in Tokyo, there was a part of me that found an accent on a woman exotic. It made me feel like they belonged to other men, and I found it sexually arousing. But I couldn't possibly mention that.

'In the collection . . .'

'Yes.'

'I'm sorry.'

'For what?'

'That my explanation is taking so long. It really isn't all that interesting.'

'That's no problem. Please go ahead. I have more time on my hands than I know what to do with.'

'Poetry. I'm embarrassed. And at my age too.'

'It's nothing to be embarrassed about. When I was young I also dabbled in my fair share, or perhaps more than my fair share . . .'

'Of poetry?'

'Yes.'

'You used to write your own?'

'No. But I read poems.'

'I see.'

'Though now that I've been working in sales for almost twenty-five years, I feel that old me is long gone.'

'Have you changed that much?'

'Oh, I've changed,' I said, and felt immediately embarrassed, like I was giving her some sort of sweet talk. 'Not that I'm disappointed that I've changed,' I added unnecessarily.

The woman was silent.

'So whose poem was it? Was it part of an anthology?'

'I too . . .'

'Huh?'

'I too have changed,' said the woman.

'You'd be a ghost if you hadn't.'

What a stupid thing for me to say. I should have gone with the flow of her feelings.

But the woman did not seem to be upset by my words.

'Poems,' she said again, 'it's been such a long time since I last read one. I wonder why I suddenly mentioned it now.'

'Maybe it's the effect of being in a hospital. I'm the same way. Lying here, away from work, I feel my forgotten self slowly resurfacing.'

'It's not that long ago.'

'What isn't?'

'The poem.'

'Oh, I see.'

'When I went home to Yokohama, I saw it in the newspaper. In a small section that quotes a poem every day.'

'"Occasional Verse".'

'No, not that. But something like it.'

'I see.'

'An eighty-year-old father . . .'

'Yes.'

'Is lying sick in bed, his mind no longer clear . . .'

'I see.'

'And he suddenly shouts, "Mother". Or perhaps it was "Ma".'

'Yes.'

'It's frightening.'

'Huh?'

'To think what I would say in the same situation.'

'Right.'

I could understand very well how she felt. I wondered what women would say in those instances? What was she afraid she might say? The name of a man other than her husband? Is that what she was trying to tell me? If so, it would have been an insult.

'Talking to myself.'

'Pardon?'

'The idea reminded me of the poem.'

'I see . . .'

'The phrase that slips out the most is, "I hate it."'

'When you talk to yourself?'

'Yes. I often say, "I hate it."'

She had told me this just moments after she'd said she didn't want me to hear the words she'd let slip.

'Is that what you said earlier?'

'No, that was something else.'

'What was is it you said then?'

'I can't tell you.'

It all seemed a little ridiculous, but I didn't think it would be appropriate to end the conversation on that note, so I asked, 'What do you hate?'

'Everything. Anything and everything.'

Perhaps she was younger than I had thought she was.

'Mr Taura . . .'

The woman said my name. It made my heart miss a beat. She

knew my name because the nurse had introduced us earlier, but I felt like the anonymous world divided by the partition had been shattered. What was her surname again? I couldn't remember. Perhaps I hadn't wanted to remember it. An unconscious excuse to my wife as I was going to be alone with a woman, although this was out of necessity and not because I was interested in the woman. Or perhaps I wanted to eliminate anything earthly from this strange night spent separated from a woman by a flimsy partition.

'Pardon?' I asked, unable to make out what the woman had said.

'I said, when you talk to yourself, what kind of things do you say?'

'Me?'

'Yes.'

'What kind of things . . .'

I hesitated for a moment.

'I'm sorry,' the woman apologised immediately. 'You wouldn't want to share it, would you?' She let out a small laugh and said, 'What am I doing, acting all bubbly. Asking such a thing?'

I detected a quiver in her voice as if she was about to cry and it made me feel the womanliness in her.

'I really don't mind,' I said, to soothe her, but in truth I did feel slightly annoyed. It was typical woman's talk – blaming herself, then feeling sorry for herself.

'I didn't get the feeling that you were acting bubbly. Were you?'

'Well, I don't usually talk this much.'

'You've been in a private room for longer than I have. It's no surprise that you're talking a little more than usual.'

'I should go to sleep now . . .'

'Sure, if you like.'

'Yes . . .'

'Let's do that then.'

'All right . . .'

We were left with an unsettling feeling – as if we had suddenly cut our conversation short. Then once again, I could hear the sound of the repair work in the distance.

'Excuse me . . .' I said.

'Pardon?'

'I'm going to use the urine bottle before going to sleep.'

'Of course.'

'Sorry. I don't really know what I'm supposed to do in these situations.'

'Well, I guess these kinds of situations rarely present themselves.'

'That's true.' A man and woman with their beds so close together . . .

'Please go ahead.'

'Okay.'

I found it funny that I had gotten her permission to go and I let out a small laugh. She did too. Conscious of the sound I would be making, I was unable to get anything out. And perhaps out of consideration, she began creating some noise by fixing her bed. I tried to go while she was doing this, but I couldn't let it out in time.

Tinkle, tinkle. The desire that wells up at the thought that a woman was listening to that sound. Was it sadism? Or masochism?

'Tinkle, tinkle,' I said. 'There's this famous poem called "Washbasin".'

'By Mitsuharu Kaneko.'

'Do you know it?'

'Yes . . .'

It was a poem about prostitutes in Guangdong, China. The preface described how the women straddle a washbasin in front of their customers and urinate with a 'tinkle, tinkle'.

'It starts out, in the washbasin, a lonesome sound,' I said.

'You're right,' she said.

As I put the urine bottle away, I continued.

'Pools of rain, a Tanjung evening.'

How strange. It had been twenty-seven or twenty-eight years since I'd read that. It had been buried deep down in my memories and I hadn't remembered it at all until now.

'It reverberates endlessly in my stirring, sinking, tired heart.'

I was able to continue smoothly.

'As long as life continues.

'You should listen.

'To the loneliness of the sound in the washbasin.'

'You remember it well,' she said.

'Yes.'

I was surprised myself. It was strange that I did remember it so well. But at the same time I was pleased that I was able to recite a poem smoothly in front of a woman.

'I can't believe that I have to make this sound in front of a woman I've known for only four or five hours,' I said, admittedly feeling a slight frisson of pleasure.

'And then to recite a poem about urinating. Terrible if you think about it,' I continued.

'Absolutely,' said the woman, but she did seem to be enjoying it. I felt like we had become a little closer.

'I say, "Aargh"', I said.

'"Aargh" as in . . .?'

'When I talk to myself. That's what I say most often,' I said cheerfully.

'You say "Aargh" to yourself,' she said, in a similarly jovial manner.

'That's right. You know, maybe you've seen someone on a train say "Aargh" unconsciously? Well, I do that. Doesn't it happen to you?'

'It does, actually.'

'You say "Aargh"?'

'Yes. I suddenly remember something I can't stand, say "Aargh", then despise myself and feel like I can't do anything to make things better.'

The woman's voice was cheerful, however, and it made me chatter on.

'I'm not my usual self today. Reciting a poem, of all things.'

'Is it a bad thing?'

'I'll probably be muttering to myself later.'

'Why?'

'Out of embarrassment.'

'What's so embarrassing?'

'It's just not like me, that's all.'

'You think so? From your voice, I wouldn't have thought so at all.'

'I'm a deputy director of a prefab company.'

'So does that mean you can't recite poetry?'

'I was just surprised. I didn't know I had that poem memorised.'

'That's wonderful.'

The woman's voice bounced, making her seem like a different person from the one I'd first talked to and I felt a piercing desire to remove the partition.

'Anyway, we shouldn't be doing this,' I said.

'Shouldn't be doing what?' she asked.

'Well, we said we were going to go to sleep, but here we are talking again.'

'It's like a night on a school trip.'

'You did that sort of thing?' I asked.

'What you mean, "that sort of thing"?'

'I mean, with boys, like this.'

'Of course not,' she laughed. 'I went to an all-girls school.'

'Oh, I see.'

'I just felt it would be a shame to go to sleep . . .'

Then she suddenly fell silent before adding in a soft voice, 'What am I saying?'

'No, you're right,' I said quickly. 'I think it would be a shame to go to sleep too.'

She stayed silent.

'I mean, there's no reason to make ourselves go to sleep. We'll probably be saying goodbye tomorrow. We can sleep as much as we like then.'

'I,' said the woman, 'really do feel it would be a shame to go to sleep.'

'I feel the same way. Perhaps because we get along.'

'I remembered feeling this way before. And I was trying to recall when.'

'Yes.'

'Going back in time. A long, long way back. And I realised that it was a school trip. And that's why I mentioned it.'

'I had the same experience. Throwing pillows and stuff.'

'But it's strange, isn't it?'

'What is?'

'Normally, you would expect to have those kinds of memories with a lover or husband but . . .' The woman's voice fell.

'It's hard for men and women to reach the point that they are so caught up in conversation that they don't want to go to sleep. They take a step further before they get there. My memory is with friends also. Talking with friends from school and feeling what a shame it would be to fall asleep. It's that feeling.'

'Talking in bed . . .' she went on, 'that never happened. Just being held, moving our bodies . . .'

I couldn't say anything in response. Was it the partition that made her say such a thing to a man she didn't even know? Was it the insensitivity of a middle-aged woman?

Once again, I heard the sound of metal moving in the distance.

'I know what you mean.' I finally opened my mouth and realised that the woman had become silent. 'I mean, my wife accused me of the same thing once. It seems that men are like that. It doesn't necessarily mean that your husband is cold.'

'I'm going to do it,' she said softly, as if she were reading something.

'Sorry?'

'Earlier, you said you hadn't heard. What I had mumbled to myself.'

'Yes.'

'I said, "I'm going to do it."'

Do what? It seemed like it would be an appropriate question to ask. But what if she was talking about murder, for example? If that was the case, I thought I'd maybe better keep my mouth shut than risk unleashing some limitless animosity.

'When I say "do it",' she continued, 'I'm not clear about exactly what it is I want to do. But something to betray my husband. Something to push my husband away. To alarm him . . .'

'I see . . .'

'But . . .'

'Yes?'

'But in reality, those kinds of strong feelings towards my husband, they disappeared a long time ago. The habit of speaking to myself, on the other hand, that still remains.'

She let out a deep sigh, as if trying to regain her calm. Someone shuffled past in the corridor, dragging their slippers. A door creaked, then the sound of them changing into wooden bathroom sandals.

'Will you do it for me?' asked the woman quietly, bringing my attention back to the room.

I looked at the partition.

'Do what?'

'Me. Will you please do me?'

The blue cloth, the only colour in this dark room, stayed completely still, but I could tell she was watching me, that her body would be very close to mine if the partition were removed. I could feel something like the weight of the situation and I let out a small laugh, as if letting out a breath.

'You're such a tease. For a second there I thought you were serious.'

'I am serious.'

'But how would we do it? Neither of us can move.'

'This kind of thing has never happened before. To be like this with someone other than my husband.'

'It could happen any time if you feel like it.'

'Really? Does this kind of thing happen to you often?'

'Of course not. To be sleeping like this with someone else's wife? I have to admit it doesn't happen all the time.'

'Please don't be offended. And please don't think that I am teasing. Because I'm not.'

'But I can't move.'

'You're right. That must be why I can say such a thing.'

'Oh, I see,' I sighed. 'You surprised me,' I said with a light laugh.

But the tone of the woman's voice didn't change.

'I have no intention of teasing or making fun of you.'

'To say something like that to an immobile man *is* teasing in a way.'

'Does it sound like I'm teasing you?'

'No, it doesn't. But you could be.'

'Men are so cautious. They don't like to be teased.'

'And women? They like it?'

'Listen, I'm not teasing. And I don't think I'm out of my mind either.'

'Well, I want to oblige, but there's nothing I can do.'

'Isn't there?' she said, urging me on. But I couldn't tell what she was urging me to do. I looked at the partition. Could she possibly be telling me to ignore my injury and come over? I felt like I could see her white face through the light blue cloth. Feel a pair of strong eyes looking at me. Though in reality I couldn't see anything.

'The partition,' I said. 'Would you mind if I moved it?'

I wanted to see her beautiful face. I'd got the feeling she was beautiful.

'No. I don't want that. On no account . . .' Her voice was thin, but had a firmness that made my heart leap. 'Please, with your voice.'

'My voice?'

'Yes, with your voice. I'm going to bare my breasts now.'

I could hear her pushing away her blankets. Feel her hastily unbuttoning her top. My excitement suddenly faded. But hearing her breathing and the slight but hurried movement of the blankets made me question my falling interest and I didn't want to embarrass her either. Part of me hated myself for feeling this way.

'My breasts,' her voice shivered. 'Will you caress them?'

'Sure, okay.' My words were clumsy. But I couldn't immediately immerse myself in her world.

'I'm stretching out my right hand,' I said, though my voice sounded dull to me.

'Yes,' replied the woman.

'I'm going to touch your right breast.'

'Yes.'

'Beautiful.' I felt momentarily flustered, wishing to say something more fitting.

'Your clear white skin . . .' I continued.

'Yes.'

'Your nipples . . .'

'Yes.'

'I'm squeezing one of them now.' I reminded myself I mustn't laugh. That I should try to become intoxicated in the situation. I heard her let out a deep breath. Heard her massaging her breasts. I didn't know what to say, but listened intently to the repetition of her heavy breathing.

Trying not to shatter that world, I told her, 'I don't know what I'm supposed to say.'

'It's okay. You don't have to say anything.'

'I wish I knew what to say.'

'It's okay, you can stay silent.'

I listened to her breathing.

'I want to see,' I said.

'No.'

'But I want to.'

I touched the partition.

'No.' Her voice came back sharp. 'No.'

I pulled my hand back.

'I'm sorry,' she said.

'No, it's okay . . .'

'I mean, this way. Because we are like this, we can do things that would be embarrassing otherwise . . .'

'We men,' I said apologetically. 'We sometimes fear we're misunderstanding the words of women. We sometimes wonder whether to take their words at face value.'

'I really don't want you to do that.'

'Are you baring just your breasts?'

'Yes.'

'Can you take off your clothes from your waist down?'

'No. But . . .'

'You could slide your hand in.'

'Yes.'

'I want to slide my hand in.'

'Yes.'

'Is your hair thick?'

'No. If anything . . .'

'Delicately thin.'

'Yes.'

'Ah, you're right. You can open your legs a little, can't you?'

'I'll try.'

'You have to make it easier for me to touch you properly.'

'Yes.'

I couldn't get swept away by the moment. If anything, I needed to stay on guard. Afraid that it would all feel dull again if I let my guard down, I pulled out my wet fingers, pushed my body up against hers and pushed myself in. She let out a cry. I pushed in deeper and deeper. I told her I had come, voiced my ecstasy, and in reality I came into tissues. It had been a long while and my sexual urges had lain dormant for several months.

* * *

Around six-thirty the next morning I heard footsteps in the hallway and the door opened.

'Good morning,' said the head nurse. Then she opened the door all the way and a rolling bed was pushed in.

'That's not going to work,' the head nurse scolded, and the bed was immediately pulled back out into the hallway.

'Can't get it in?' asked a man's voice.

Without responding to him, the head nurse immediately came back into the room, smiled and said, 'We're going to move you.' Then she bent down as if she were looking under the bed.

'This bed is on wheels, so we're going to release the brakes and move it.'

'Oh, it's one of those,' said the young nurse who had been on night duty, as she bent over and looked under the bed.

'Release the wheels,' said the head nurse.

'Where am I being moved to?' I asked.

'Room 501,' said the head nurse, standing up, like she was stating the obvious.

The nurse who had been on night duty bumped her backside against the partition and turned round.

'Well, I guess we don't need this any more,' she said, putting a hand on the metal frame of the partition. I heard a cry, and then I saw her before my eyes.

'Is something the matter?' asked the young nurse as she pushed the partition to the foot of the bed. The woman had closed her eyes and turned her face away. But I could see her grey hair and trembling profile. She was old.

'What's the matter?' asked the head nurse.

'Nothing,' the woman said, resigned. Her eyes were closed and the image of her grey hair and the wrinkled, lifeless skin around her cheeks burned itself into my mind.

2

About a month and a half after that, I was transferred to the
built-to-order projects department at Tokyo Headquarters. It
had only six staff members and so felt more like a household
than a department, with the department director, myself, three
other permanent employees and a woman on a one-year contract. The department had been established by our chairman,
who had passed away the previous summer, and was, in reality,
a kind of refuge for people determined by the company to be in
no condition to work on the front line.

With the exception of Mr Imori, a guy in his mid thirties
from the Tsuda branch who considered himself a temporary
member while recovering from an operation for a duodenal
ulcer, the other four employees, including the department
director, had on at least one occasion displayed their mental
condition too obviously to cover up. I myself, just as we were
about to win a contract for a temporary junior high-school
building, had skipped a dinner with the Board of Education
arranged by my department's assistant manager, and jumped
out of the second-floor window of a sushi restaurant.

Taking into consideration my prior contribution to the company, and for fear of the emotional distress that a demotion
would cause, I was given the position and benefits of a deputy
director. The others in the department were also given section-

head or assistant-manager level compensation. The departmental director explained to me that this was due to the compassion of the executives, who thought that we would remain blind to the reality of our situations if given these titles. The director didn't harbour any antipathy toward the 'naïve compassion' of the executives. As far as he was concerned, compassion was compassion, and we should be grateful for it. 'It's a real luxury,' said the director in a preachy tone.

The assistant manager-by-title told me later that the director was trying to be like the head of a religious organisation he frequented when he said that. He would talk endlessly about how it was a 'real luxury' for the company to 'assign a girl' to a department with no real work, and how it was out of the president's respect for the chairman that the department would remain untouched for at least one year after his passing. So even though our department might not last long, 'we must be grateful and never take the kindness shown us for granted'. I didn't need to be told not to take our situation for granted and I had no intention of doing so. But we had no work, because in reality the business development department managed the built-to-order projects and they 'didn't want people who had lost their minds getting in the way'.

Our director accepted the way things were done. So in the end, all we had to do was to kill time and refrain from acting important. As a result, the person who acted the most self-important was the female contract employee, Yoshiko Takamatsu, who was the youngest at thirty-one but who would scold the director, saying, 'You never use the tea saucer, no matter how many times I tell you.'

'Mr Taura!' It was Yoshiko Takamatsu calling out my name in

a grumpy voice one afternoon in early March.

'Yes?'

'How many times do I need to call your name?'

'You called my name that many times?'

'Yes. "Mr Taura", "Mr Taura", I said.'

'That's twice.'

'No. I called you once again after that.'

'What is it?'

'Phone call.'

'For me?'

'Would I call your name if it was for someone else?'

Of course not, but it was very rare for me to receive a phone call. It wasn't that the people around me treated me coldly, but rather a case of me avoiding people myself. I found phone calls to be a nuisance.

'Hello?'

'Mr Taura?'

Anger was a rare emotion for me around that time, but the nausea that rose to my throat when I heard that voice was something very close to it. I couldn't believe that she would even think of calling me. After moving beds that day, I'd made no attempt to go near or learn about her. I felt that no matter what I did, I would end up hurting her. The woman I had seen at the hospital was unmistakably an old woman. I had momentarily been hit by a terrible feeling of disgust when I found out, but once I'd had time to think about it, I'd decided that it wasn't her fault she had aged. I was even able in a way to understand why she would want to take advantage of the partition to pretend she was younger than she was. It must have been a worse experience for her than for me and I didn't want to do anything to aggravate the situation. I felt that even just asking after her health would do so. That to have no contact with her whatsoever, to forget about her, would help her save face. But at the same time, though I wasn't about to ask where she was from and what her background was, I *was* curious about how old she actually was – being clearly over sixty yet pretending to be, and sounding, much younger. I kept this curiosity to myself, however. There was also a part of me that felt a slight sense of satisfaction in taking what I thought was the most mature course of action. When I'd left the hospital in mid January, I didn't even know if she was still in the hospital. And when I stood outside the hospital and looked up at the window of what had been my room, I avoided shifting my glance to room 513.

I had done this out of consideration for her, and I had thought that she must have sensed it at least a little. But to give me a call? That wasn't something I'd be able to do if I was in her position. I'd be far too embarrassed.

'Taura speaking,' I said, trying to keep my voice void of emotion.

'My name is Miyabayashi. We were together at the hospital.'

How insensitive of her to choose those words, 'we were together'. Didn't she have the sense to avoid words that might allude to what had happened?

'Hello?'

'Yes.'

'Do you remember me?'

Her voice was young. So even after having seen what she looked like, I couldn't imagine that she was an old woman after hearing her voice again.

'Hello?' she said in her young voice.

'Yes.'

'Do you . . . remember . . .?'

'I remember. Of course,' I said, as if to push her words back. How could I possibly forget? I had been dragged into it and she'd even made me come. How could she think that I could have forgotten?

'Well, I'm calling from a public phone in the Mitsui building.'

What did that have to do with me?

'And I was wondering, if you were going to finish work at five, if I could see you.'

It was already past four.

'I'm afraid that I have to work late today. If you will excuse me, I'm in a meeting.'

I ended the call abruptly.

'There was a time when I used to say that kind of thing,' said the section head-by-title with a nostalgic expression.

'You shouldn't have,' said the director. 'You mustn't avoid meeting people. You should meet them, even if you have to make yourself.'

'Yes, but this was a special case.'

'A debt collector, perhaps?' said Yoshiko Takamatsu. You could see in her expression that she thought she'd said something witty.

'Are you in debt?' asked the director.

'Of course, I am. With a company loan and a mortgage, just like everybody else.'

'But people don't come around collecting on those.'

'I simply meant that it was someone I needed to avoid.'

'Are women to be avoided?' Takamatsu shared her unwelcome opinion.

'Certainly,' said the section head-by-title. 'With the exception of you, of course.'

'Was it a woman?' asked the director. 'If that's the case, you *have* to see her.'

'As the deputy director's proxy, I'll volunteer to see her instead,' said the assistant manager-by-title.

Everyone politely laughed and I looked over at Imori, who was looking glum. I found myself almost automatically suppressing the disgust I felt at everything around me.

Then, at twenty past five, I got up and left the office.

I was the last one to leave, so I locked up and gave the key to the landlord, who had an optician's shop on the first floor. I didn't need to leave it with him, but if I didn't then I couldn't be late the next morning. Not that that had ever happened.

Our office was in an old four-storey building that stood between the Koshu Highway and the Shinjuku high-rises. We were renting the third floor, while the main department of our head office was located in a skyscraper elsewhere.

I headed for the station, all the while slightly worried in case the woman had been waiting for me on the street (that was why I had delayed my departure), but there seemed to be no sign of her. Why on earth did she want to see me? I just couldn't understand women. Sometimes I had felt my wife was unbearably 'other' or alien to me. But if it had been my wife in such a situation, she would never have suggested a meeting. If anything, she would have harboured hatred towards the man.

The woman had said that her family home was in Yokohama, just outside Tokyo, and I wondered who lived in her family home. That's where she must have been visiting. Her reason for being in town.

I had to use the pedestrian bridge. I could have avoided using it, but that would have meant taking the long way round. The section head-by-title had once said that you could tell how young you were by which route you chose, and our office spent half a day arguing which route meant you were younger. I had argued, despite having no firm reason, that you were younger if you chose to use the pedestrian bridge and had stuck by that position ever since. The assistant manager-by-title, on the other hand, had claimed that 'stairs were tough on old people'. He might have been right. Perhaps a flat route would be easier even if it were longer.

It wasn't a particularly busy bridge, but at a little after five a stream of pedestrians would generally form on it. I walked along with the flow of people towards Shinjuku.

'Mr Taura.' A woman's voice called from behind. She was right behind me. I didn't stop. I kept walking as if I hadn't heard her.

'Mr Taura.'

It would have been only natural to turn round and I noticed a man walking next to me shoot me a glance. But I didn't stop. I kept walking. Maintaining my pace. The woman stopped calling my name. But I didn't sense her stopping. She was probably walking right behind me. What was she up to? What did she think she would get out of meeting after all this time? Couldn't she sense how I felt? As I walked down the stairs I was hit by a burst of rage. What was she thinking? If she'd left it as it was, it might even have become a sad but beautiful memory. I quickened my pace a little, and when I reached the bottom of the staircase I turned round. Immediately behind me was a middle-aged man. I looked to see who was behind him, but I didn't see anybody like her. Again, I felt I'd been teased and I quickly moved away from the stairs, away from the glances of strangers.

As I stepped away, I thought I glimpsed a woman in the corner of my field of vision. I turned round and looked up to see a woman in a kimono standing on the right corner at the top of the stairs. People walked past her and down. She watched me silently, oblivious to the flow of people. My mouth may have dropped open a little. She was not an old woman. She looked like she was in her forties. She bowed. I bowed back. But it wasn't an old woman, so it couldn't have been the woman from that time. She was definitely looking at me, though; she'd bowed at me and the voice that called my name was the same as the one that night. She began descending the stairs slowly. Did this mean the old woman was going to appear from behind her? Maybe not; she was alone. And there was no grey in her hair. But hair can be dyed. And how about her skin? That can be disguised with make-up, too. Though it'd take a pretty heavy application to transform that lady into this one. And anyway, she didn't seem to be wearing that much make-up.

'I'm Miyabayashi,' said the woman.

It was the same voice as that time.

'Right . . .'

'I'm sorry for waiting for you without your permission.'

'That's all right.'

Face to face, I realised she was slightly smaller than me. Although her skin was nothing like the aged skin I remembered, she had small wrinkles at the corners of her eyes.

'I'm Taura . . .'

'I'm sorry, I . . . please excuse me.'

She bowed her head again. After my thoughts had left her

skin and hair, I realised my anger had melted away. In fact, it had begun to fade as soon as I saw her at the top of the stairs. I was surprised by the pleasant appearance of this woman approaching in her elegant, striped kimono and, though I didn't know anything about kimonos, I thought she looked very refined and that she exuded no sense of working in the bar business with which kimonos are often associated. She didn't appear to be particularly gaunt, but after seeing her face I did wonder a little if she was perhaps just a bit too thin. But with her big eyes and lips I imagined she'd have given the impression of being a sharp woman when she was younger. There were, however, little traces of middle-age weight gain here and there that lent a slight softening effect to her appearance.

'If you could spare just a little time for me,' she said, 'perhaps we can go for some tea.'

Declining her offer didn't even cross my mind.

'At this time of day, the closer we go to the station the more packed places are going to be. We should maybe backtrack a little.'

We began walking back towards the cluster of skyscrapers. I knew a few places that probably wouldn't be that crowded even at that time of day, and there were also a few right behind my office, but I found myself choosing a nice place in one of the skyscrapers that I had been to just once before.

I searched for words as we walked. There were plenty of things to talk about if I asked questions, but those that came to my mind seemed somehow inappropriate to ask while walking.

'How long have you been here?' I asked, thinking that this would not be intruding too much.

'It must be about a month now.'

'That long . . .'

'I'm not going back home.'

The way she said 'not going back home' made it seem that she still had a home to go back to. I felt that I might be intruding by continuing the conversation, so I didn't, and we continued to walk in silence. I found myself wondering if an illness could transform such a beautiful person into an old woman. It was hard to believe that anyone could regain their youth to this extent in just three months after recovering from an illness.

I occasionally matched my steps to hers and slipped glances at her. Sometimes she would keep looking forward and sometimes she would shoot a quick smile back. It couldn't be true. No matter how many times I retraced my memory, the person I had seen that morning was an old woman. Her hair was thin and grey, and I couldn't possibly forget the deep wrinkles in her ashen skin. The two couldn't possibly be the same, could they? Perhaps it was her daughter. It was not unusual for mother and daughter to have similar voices. And there was nothing about the woman walking next to me, other than her voice, that resembled the old lady at the hospital. It was true that I had caught only a glimpse of her face then, but it wasn't as if I had heard about her from someone else, or that I'd had a premonition about her. Although only a glance, I had seen with my own two eyes that she was old. If the woman next to me suddenly fell ill, would she turn into that person again? It was especially hard to believe that a lumbar fracture could do that. Was this some kind of trick? But what would anyone have to gain from fooling someone like me?

'It's on the third floor,' I said.

'I see.'

'The second floor is a shopping promenade, but the third floor is mostly offices, so I thought the place might be quite empty.'

I pushed the heavy door open.

'You're right,' said the woman in a small voice.

It wasn't a big place, though it was luxuriously appointed. There were only three groups of customers and it was surprisingly quiet compared to the stores on the second floor.

'Just one floor makes such a difference,' I said.

'It certainly does.'

She faced me and gave me a nod in which I somehow sensed someone older. But she couldn't have been older. I was forty-eight. And she couldn't have been older than forty-two or forty-three, although it is hard to tell the age of a beautiful woman. Who knows, she might actually have been around the same age as me, I thought. Entranced by her beauty, I didn't want to think that there was any plot or deception behind this. Then, after ordering coffee, I told her what had been on my mind. 'I should have said this earlier,' I told her, 'but when you called I was in a meeting. So please forgive me for having been on edge.'

The woman gave a slight bow in response. 'No, I should apologise for calling you at work.'

'I'm just curious,' I said. 'How were you able to find me?'

'You mentioned at the hospital that you worked at your company's Northern Japan branch office.'

'No, I meant how you called out to me on the footbridge. You didn't see me at the hospital.'

'I saw you.'

'When?'

'When you were leaving the hospital. I saw you from the window.'

But it must have been a fifth-floor window.

'And you could recognise me from that?'

'Not only that.'

'I don't mean to press you, but . . .'

'I went to your home.'

'In Kitami?'

'Yes.'

Kitami was a small station near the Tama River on the Odakyu Line. I had built a home about a fifteen-minute walk from that station six years ago.

'Yesterday I saw you come home.'

'So it must have already been night-time.'

'It was light enough to tell what you looked like.'

'So why didn't you say something?'

'That would have been an inconvenience for you, would it not?'

It was true that I didn't really want to have to explain the situation to my wife. But it didn't seem normal to come to my house and see me, then leave without saying a word.

'The forsythias in your garden were blooming nicely.'

'Yes, they are. Thank you.'

'And such a nice house.'

'You're too kind . . .'

My wife didn't like the prefabricated homes of our company so we had spent a little more on our house than we should have. It was built of wood and had cost about 30,000 yen more per square metre than a prefab house would have. I didn't think our company's homes were all that bad, so I was a little hurt when my wife said that she didn't want a prefab house. But at the same time, I felt that by choosing a prefab home, I would be leaving a mark of my achievements in the form of a home and so decided to go along with my wife. Now I couldn't care less.

'That morning . . .' the woman started. 'That morning at the hospital.'

'Yes.'

'You must have been disgusted.'

' . . . No.'

'Pretending to be young, thinking that we would never see each other.'

'You are young in reality.'

'But you didn't think so when you saw me that morning, did you?'

'No. There were some grey streaks in your hair.'

'Not some. My whole head was grey.'

'I have heard that these things can happen.'

'These things?'

'That people can turn grey overnight due to an illness or stress – even though they are still young.'

'It's not like that.'

'Side effects from medication, maybe?'

'No.'

Then what was it? I almost asked, but I didn't, thinking that she might not want to talk about it. She changed the subject.

'After leaving the hospital, I separated from my husband.'

She said these words without any sadness, as if she were just stating facts.

'That's why you are at your family home in Yokohama . . .'

'You remember that it's in Yokohama . . .'

'You did mention it.'

'I didn't think you would remember such a minor detail.'

'Well, it's very rare to have a night like that.'

'But I'm not at my family home. My brother died last year, so the only people living there are his wife, the eldest son, the son's wife and their children.'

'So you live alone . . .'

'Yes.'

The coffee came.

'I . . .'

She waited for the waiter to leave and looked up.

'Yes.'

She dropped her gaze abruptly and let out a small sigh as if she was hesitating to voice her thoughts.

'Is there something?'

'Yes,' she nodded, and said, 'I've become young again.'

I could see that, obviously.

'My hair isn't dyed,' she said, touching her head.

'Well, I think I should keep this information classified,' I said, smiling.

'Classified?'

'Yes, a secret.'

'Keep what a secret?'

'Well if middle-aged women found out that they could all become much younger by leaving their husbands, they'd do it without a second thought.'

She laughed and said, 'You know how I don't have anybody—'

'Nobody?'

'Like friends . . .'

'Even in Yokohama?'

'I have friends I haven't seen for a long time, but things aren't so simple. I can't just go and see them.'

'Why not?'

'Because I've become younger.'

'But that's a good thing.'

'Even so, I would imagine they'd find it creepy.'

'Of course they wouldn't. You should show off your youth.'

'I suddenly realised that there was only you . . .'

'But it was just one night . . .'

'It was a first for me, and I had a good time.'

'I had a good time as well.'

'But because I pretended to be young . . .'

'You can't say it was pretending.'

'You must have felt like you had been taken in, and I was feeling very sorry about that. I also thought that it was very kind of you to act like you had forgotten about it afterwards.'

'To be honest with you, the whole experience was beginning to feel like a dream to me. It's not a bad memory. A kind of sweet–'

'Me too.'

'When you called, I was afraid that memory would be ruined. I wanted to keep that experience as it was.'

'I'm sorry,' she said, bowing her head.

'No. Now that we've met, I'm glad we did.'

'I'm selfish.'

'No.'

'You know how you saw me as a grey-haired old woman. Once I became younger, I wanted you to see me like this.'

'I'm not very smooth with words, but you are beautiful.'

'But I hesitated. I thought that it would be an inconvenience to you. Going to your home.'

'That a woman would get nervous over seeing me at this age?' I said. 'I can't help but let it go to my head.'

'What time are you free until?' she asked, glancing at the clock.

'Any time. I don't work overtime these days. It's a good thing to stay out late once in a while.'

The fact that I didn't work overtime meant I didn't get any overtime pay and that I couldn't afford to go out, so I almost always ate at home. My wife and son were often out, but there would be something waiting for me that I could just heat up on the stove or in the microwave. I would turn on the TV and eat dinner with the 7:30 shows like *Word Association Game* and *Quiz Derby* as my companions.

'Let's celebrate our recoveries!' I said, my voice becoming a little louder.

I was worried about my budget, but I had a good idea of what things would cost in this area, so I felt I'd be able to manage.

After that, things gradually started to become clear. The Japanese restaurant in the basement of the same building had no free tables and the zashiki-style rooms were all reserved. We were told that there were seats at the counter, but there was a group of men in their thirties and forties who were already slightly drunk.

'I think it'll be fine,' she said.

'No, let's go up to another floor.'

On the forty-fourth floor we switched lifts to the one that went all the way up to the fifty-fifth. I didn't want to make her walk so much if possible, but if we had sat at the counter, those men would have no doubt started ogling her. And ever since moving back from the Northern Japan branch office, I'd had an aversion towards energetic-looking office workers.

'If you could just wait for a short while,' said the greeter at the restaurant on the fifty-fourth floor.

Then we were taken to the bar where we sat with the night view to our backs. I ordered a Martini and she opted for a Campari soda. I caught the middle-aged Caucasian couple sitting next to us whispering to each other.

'Beautiful.'

'Really is.'

Wondering what they were praising, I glanced at them as I put my hand towel down. The grey-haired husband smiled at me as if to say, 'Maybe you overheard us?' Then he looked me sincerely in the eyes, as if he were about to confess something.

'Excuse me, but since coming to Tokyo, we've rarely seen anyone in a kimono. I think this is the first time I have come to really understand the beauty of a kimono.'

The wife, who was sitting on the other side of the husband, nodded enthusiastically.

'I'm one of those people who normally think kimono designs are lacking in taste, but I'd love one with a refined fabric like that.'

I said 'thank you' to them and turned back to the woman. Her eyes were asking, *What did they say?* And when I told her what they had said, she looked at the couple, smiled and said, 'Thank you very much,' in a small voice. The couple nodded, then left us alone.

Our drinks were placed in front of us.

'It's true.'

'What is?'

'Their remarks.'

'Well, I have to say, that I'm quite fond of this myself.'

'It's not the kimono.'

'No. It's the kimono,' she said.

'No.'

I was about to seriously tell her how beautiful she was, but the bartender came close by.

'Bon appétit.' She picked up her glass a little quickly as if to escape my compliments.

'Yes—'

That's when I finally realised and turned pale.

How had I understood the couple?

They'd spoken to me in French. But I'd been able to understand them quite easily and had interpreted for her, too. This couldn't be possible. Even though I'd chosen French as my second foreign language at university, I'd only ever studied very basic textbooks and had forgotten most of it anyway. Even if I *had* been able to understand the conversation I'd just had, surely I would have had to ask them to repeat what they'd said several times, perhaps even with some English, and it would have still taken me some time to digest. There was no way I would have been able to understand what they had said so easily.

'Are you talking to yourself?' asked the woman.

'What?'

'You said, "Ah."'

'Just now?'

'Yes.'

'No, it's—'

I didn't think I had voiced my thoughts.

'We drank our drinks without making a toast,' I said, moving the conversation forward.

'I still have some left.'

'I guess I'll have another then.'

I asked the bartender for another of the same. Then I was suddenly overcome with an unsuppressible need to talk to the Caucasian man again.

'When did you arrive in Japan?'

I could speak French.

'Three, no, four days now.'

'I see.'

I must have learned that level of French in class. But . . .

'Your French is very good,' whispered the woman by my ear.

'It shouldn't be.'

'No, it's excellent.'

'I've been in Tokyo the entire time,' said the white man. My wife's been to Kamakura and Hakone on a bus tour, but I had business to attend to.'

'Are you finished with that now?'

'Almost. When I'm done, I plan to go and see Kyoto and Himeji Castle.'

'That's nice.'

'Although my friends who know a lot about Japan tell me those aren't the best sites to see.' I couldn't catch what he said next. I guess there were words I didn't understand, too. It was not surprising, given that I really shouldn't have been able to understand hardly a word, but there was a part of me that was puzzled by the fact that this miracle had its limits.

I gave him a vague smile. 'You should go to Kyoto,' I said.

'We plan to,' said the husband with a smile. The wife also smiled and nodded.

'Mr Taura,' the waiter said in a small voice behind my back, 'your table is ready.'

It was the first time I'd been to this restaurant, and the first time I'd seen the night view of skyscrapers from a window in the sky with a woman, but for some reason I felt like I was reliving the experience.

When I was thirty-seven, I began a three-year relationship with a twenty-six-year-old woman at an architectural office in Yotsuya. It was the only affair I ever had. Now, as we began eating, I could feel the same sexual desire, the same guilt, the same sense of accomplishment, and the same burden I felt back then gradually coming back to me. It wasn't a vivid, graphic memory, but one wrapped in nostalgia that nudged forward my feelings that were already leaning towards the woman.

The woman looking through the menu under the dim lights wasn't as young as the woman in my past, but she was so beautiful that I would have felt daunted by her had it not been for the unusual circumstances under which we'd met. I found the quality of her skin to be just right for someone her age, comforting even. If on top of being so beautiful, she had also been young, I would probably have felt lonely sitting there with her.

Looking back, the woman I had an affair with was a reflection of my low self-worth. But even when I was at the peak of my career, I probably wouldn't have even dared to think of having an affair with the woman in front of me now. Even more so today.

I gave our orders and our wine was brought to us. I watched her profile as she looked down at the night view of the forest of high-rises, remarking that 'the tiny lights are so beautiful', and my timid wonderings about an ulterior motive for her meeting me began flutter around my chest.

'That night,' she said. 'We only talked for a few hours, so when I think of something to talk about with you, I can only think of things about the hospital or our individual lives.'

'I know.'

'But I want to forget those things.'

'I'm all for that. I'm sure you might have guessed, but the life I lead isn't all that exciting.'

She looked me in the eyes in silence. As if she were attempting to read something in mine. I smiled without looking away.

'Then what should we talk about?' I asked.

'Anything,' she said, appearing relieved.

Perhaps it was just me, but I got the feeling that she was looking for self-pity in my eyes. But even I have some pride and I was pretty certain I wasn't revealing anything like that.

'You can't see it from here . . .' I said, turning to the night view.

'Yes.' The woman turned her gaze to the direction I was looking in.

'There's the KDD building.'

'The international phone carrier?'

'Yes, well, I suppose you could call it something like a telephone station.'

'Yes.'

'I think it's nine o'clock, that's when the international phone rates become cheap. You can see foreigners who don't have a phone at home flocking there every night to call people overseas.'

'Always the same people?'

'All kinds of people. Given that they don't have a phone at

home, I suspect most of them go once a week at most, or once a month perhaps.'

'I see . . .'

'The waiting room and phone booths are filled with all kinds of foreigners.'

'I guess so.'

'So you can hear many different languages from different far-away places. Some people are so happy to be talking to their families that they start speaking loudly without realising it. Some people start crying just saying the word 'mom'. Others receive news of someone's death. And others of birth. And there are people listening to these various voices as they sit waiting with their heads down. It seems there are always more Asians than Caucasians.'

'I see.'

'There must be men and women that meet in the waiting room.'

'I imagine so.'

I looked down at the night view.

'Their Tokyo is probably very different from our Tokyo.'

'Yes.'

She too was gazing at the glimmering windows across the city.

'That's all . . .'

'That's all it takes,' she said, 'to make the night view look completely different.'

I looked down at the stream of headlights, the river of red tail-lights going in the other direction and the people walking along the pavement here and there.

'I don't have any wonderful observations like that to share, but . . .'

She told me about an old woman in Gloucester, England, who had lost her husband. She'd read it in the paper a few years ago. The husband was eighty-one years old and weighed 120 kilograms. The wife, who was seventy-seven years old and weighed only 44 kilograms, was pinned underneath her husband. She tried to push him off, but his body wouldn't budge. She screamed, but nobody heard. It was three whole days before she was found. She spent three days under her husband's dead body. In the end, her nephew visited her house, became suspicious on seeing the uncollected milk bottles by the front door and called the police. The old woman was rescued and she recovered in hospital.

I laughed. She grinned too and said, 'That's all there is to the story.'

'That's all,' I said, 'it takes to know.'

'Takes to know what?'

I hesitated a little at her question but decided to go ahead and tell her. After all, the two of us had exchanged more private moments across a partition.

'Basically,' I said lowering my voice. 'That they were having sex.'

'No!'

'Isn't that what the episode is about?'

'He was eighty-one years old.'

'Why else would she be pinned underneath him?'

'You're right,' she said, impressed. 'It hadn't occurred to me. I just thought it was a funny story about a woman who was rescued from under her heavy husband after three days.'

'Our antennas are probably pointing in different directions. I was comparing the old man's sexual drive with mine, and you were thinking about the poor woman who was rescued. But I'm surprised you remember an article from a few years ago so—'

She dropped her gaze and I immediately apologised.

'I shouldn't have said that. We should keep reality as far away as possible.'

After that, we talked about why wild animals on land such as giraffes and zebras weren't used for food as much as sea creatures like fish. We shared our thoughts about flowers that would soon be blossoming like cherry blossoms, aronias, wisterias and peonies. And I gave her my analysis as a construction professional of the rising Tokyo land prices.

As she was drinking her demitasse coffee, she said, 'I've reserved a hotel room.'

I thought I must have misheard her.

'Pardon, . . . I—' I looked at her.

'A hotel room.'

She dropped her gaze. But I needed a little more to be sure of what she was thinking.

'Where do you live now?'

'In Tokyo.'

Those were the words I needed. But I didn't know how to react. I'd also wondered at the same time that it might be just my wishful thinking, so I simply put down my napkin and said, 'Let's go.'

'I was thinking . . .' she began saying in a small voice without moving from her seat.

'Yes?'

' . . . that I haven't been with anyone other than my husband.'

'I see,' I replied.

'But that's not exactly the case, is it?'

'What do you mean?'

'Well, I've been with you.'

'But that was just words.'

'You weren't just words.'

'That's true, but—'

I was about to smile, but the woman continued to speak with a straight face, her gaze on the table, slowly pushing out the words.

'The memory means more to me than just words.'

* * *

It was a twin bedroom on the eighteenth floor with a large window, but the view of the city was blocked by the rear of a building two or three hundred metres away. All we could see were rows of small rectangular windows. But because of the random pattern of windows with and without lights on, it didn't feel lifeless. If anything, I felt something like a distinct sorrow arising from something large and unknown.

'I come to Shinjuku every day, but I rarely see a view like this,' I said.

Looking down, I saw a car make a half-circle in front of the hotel and drive off onto the road. The light in the room went off.

'It's better this way.'

I didn't turn round but continued to look out at the night view.

'You get a better night view this way.'

She came and stood next to me in silence. Like me, she gazed out at the concrete vista.

I held her in my arms. What else was I to do? Her body stiffened, and although she didn't resist, she remained motionless as if trying to insist that it hadn't been her that had turned off the light and approached me. I held her thin shoulders and stroked her hair. I didn't rush it. There was something hot in the deep core of her chest, and I could feel it slowly melting away. I placed my lips on her forehead, then her cheeks, and then, pushing her head back slightly, placed my tongue on her neck. Then on her ears.

Time passed in silence, then she drew a deep breath and whispered, 'It was wrong of me. To have deceived you like that, that night.'

The lips that said those words responded softly to my tongue. I touched her breasts. As my hands moved clumsily, as if foiled by the kimono, she said, 'I'll undress,' in a low voice. 'I'll take it off.'

For me to write more about my sexual accomplishments would probably just make people feel unpleasant. I have no intention of bragging either, so I won't describe in detail her body or the sadness that I felt in the softness of her white skin. Or how the first time, even at this age, I came early. Or how the second time I experienced the most perfect pleasure, intensity, persistence and oneness of all the sexual experiences in my life.

Her excitement. The gentle, slow, sex we had the third time round (yes, a third time was actually possible). The closeness of it. The sweat and the sounds. Her smell. About these things too, I won't share the details with you.

Once we were all used up and lay motionless with our eyes closed, I asked the woman her name for the first time. But as soon as I asked her, I regretted it. It was obviously better not to share names. Or at least, that's what I thought she'd think, and

I immediately took back what I said.

'Never mind. It's better if I don't ask.'

'Mutsuko,' she said casually. 'Now, after my separation, I'm Mutsuko Kizuki.'

'Mutsuko, Mutsuko, Mutsuko, Mutsuko,' I murmured and placed a hand on her breast. The next moment sleep descended on me.

I had called home from the restaurant, but nobody had picked up and that thought stayed in the corner of my mind as I fell asleep. It was fine. It wouldn't be such a bad thing for me not to return home sometimes. But later, a little later, I should try calling at least one more time – to say I wouldn't be coming home – after Mutsuko has fallen asleep, I thought. But when I next opened my eyes, the bright morning light was pouring in through the gap in the curtains. And she wasn't there.

I wasn't surprised. I think I'd unconsciously been expecting it all along. After all, they do say good things are never meant to last. This feeling took deep root in me as I thought how I might have become even more unstable if she'd stayed.

It crossed my mind that I hadn't asked exactly where she lived. And that I might never see her again. It was a thought that shot a sharp feeling of regret right through me, while at the same time I felt it would be right for us never to meet again. I went down to the front desk on my way out and found the room had already been paid for.

* * *

About five days later, I was reading the paper at my desk at work in the afternoon, when I suddenly felt like something was clawing at my stomach. It wasn't that there was an article in the paper about Mutsuko. I had actually been reading an article about something that happened in the US in a small section of the paper that featured foreign newswires from agencies like UPI.

The article was about the Resh family in Columbus, Ohio. Apparently at the Resh home, furniture would move around on its own, the telephone would float up into the air, lights would go on, water would suddenly start running from the tap and so on. A local journalist went to research the story and actually saw the furniture moving around for himself. The family turned to experts to help them find out the cause, but the scientists had all given up. The article ended by saying that many similar cases have been reported in the past.

I myself had once read an article about a similar occurrence. But I hadn't given it a second thought. There was nothing I could do about it anyway. But this was an extraordinary phenomenon, something that completely defied scientific laws and evaded explanation. Not many people saw it that way, though. Most people just thought of it as a slightly strange story, then forgot all about it. In this way their grip on reality remained firm and unchallenged.

Of course, if it was something that happened far away, you couldn't blame people for treating it that way. But what if it happened to you? Would you . . . could you forget it once it had passed? Why had I been able to speak and understand French? And that woman – Mutsuko – was that old, grey-haired woman really Mutsuko? Could I honestly believe that?

Leaving these questions aside, I returned to my daily life. I was struck by apathy, and before long it had overwhelmed me. I glanced at the phone. I thought of calling the hospital.

Mutsuko went by the last name Miyabayashi there, so I could tell them I had a question about Ms Mutsuko Miyabayashi. Then they could tell me no such person had been staying at the hospital. I felt like it was possible that would happen. But how would I ever know if I didn't call?

It wasn't really possible for me to make a private long-distance phone call from work. So I opened my diary, checked the phone number for the hospital, and, remembering that the most hard-working and cheerful nurse had been a woman named Ms Nakanobu, wrote Nakanobu under the phone number.

The whole department had been tasked to work together organising employees' opinions on how to provide diverse and detailed services for special prefab product orders, while keeping costs down at the same time. We were then to write up a 'mind-blowing' report on possible actions that might be extrapolated from this information. It was an assignment that somehow smelled of 'therapy', however. Although nobody said this out loud, it had taken any passion from the work, but even so, I couldn't just leave the office during working hours.

I decided to wait until five. In the meantime, I picked out all the 100-yen coins I had and put them in my jacket pocket. I also decided on a public phone located in a relatively quiet area. At five o'clock, as always, there were no urgent tasks waiting for me, so I left the office and went to the public phone I'd decided on.

I asked for Ms Nakanobu at the nurse's station on the fifth floor.

'My name is Taura. I was in room 501 with a fracture.'

'My, my,' Ms Nakanobu responded in a cheerful voice, just as

I had expected. 'How are you doing? Where are you calling from? From Tokyo? My–'

There was only one thing I really wanted to ask, but it would have been unnatural to ask just that, so I asked her if she knew the address of Ms Mutsuko Miyabayashi who was staying in room 513 at the end of last year.

'I have no idea.'

She told me that she could connect me to the administration office to ask there, since it was only a little past five and people should still be there.

'Then how about this? Do you know her age?' I asked quickly.

'Her age?'

'Yes, how old was she?'

'Hold on a second.'

Without showing any suspicion as to why I would be asking, she called out 'Ms Ozaki' to one of the other nurses. I couldn't hear what she said after that.

I waited. And I received the response that I had secretly been expecting.

'Ms Miyabayashi . . . sixty-seven years old.'

Just like that I found out. Perhaps it was because Mutsuko had wanted me to find out when she'd said to me, as if making a confession, 'I've become younger.' Some of the words that peppered her conversation were old-fashioned for a woman of forty-two or forty-three, too. She'd even said that her friends would be shocked if they saw how she'd become younger. Mutsuko hadn't been hiding it. I just didn't have the ability to sense the truth. I couldn't see beyond my basic assumptions. But that was no surprise.

Who could believe that a sixty-seven-year-old woman had

become that young? Who would believe such a surprising change? If anything, you would have to be losing your mind to believe such a thing so easily. So the woman I met had to be someone else. A person who, for some reason, had pretended that she was the young, rejuvenated version of the sixty-seven-year-old woman. That's why she tried to avoid questions about what had happened at the hospital and about her daily life now. But what could she possibly have to gain from doing that?

As these thoughts ran through my head, more than half of me still believed that Mutsuko really was the old woman turned younger. But this thought didn't make me feel any disgust towards her. I didn't feel the nausea or reality-shaking dizziness I'd felt when I'd seen the old woman at the hospital that morning. I was simply touched as I remembered Mutsuko's expressions, her figure and the way she'd felt as she tried to open up her younger, early forties body to me.

'Mutsuko,' I murmured under my breath as I walked. Then, in French, I tried to say, 'I want to see you.' But I couldn't find the words.

3

There were only four Kizukis in the Yokohama city phone directory and I managed to reach Mutsuko's late brother's home on the second call.

'May I ask if I am talking to a relative of a Ms Mutsuko Kizuki?'

'Yes . . .' The voice belonged to a teenage girl. A middle- or high-school student, I guessed.

'My name is Ishikawa and I'm calling from Keihin Life Insurance. I was hoping you could kindly tell me Ms Mutsuko Kizuki's address in Tokyo.'

There was a moment's silence, then the girl called for her mother. A middle-aged woman came to the phone and I introduced myself again.

'Why do you need to contact her?' she asked in an emotionless voice.

'I have information that she requested regarding the purchase of life insurance.'

'Are you saying Mutsuko bought a life-insurance policy?'

'Well, she called in to our office saying that she wanted to, but we haven't heard from her since.'

I had said this kind of thing countless times when I was working for the sales department.

'When was this?'

'About a week ago.'

The woman paused, probably in thought, then said, 'Well if she really wants to she'll probably visit you again.'

She was right, of course.

'By the way,' she continued, 'how did you get our number?'

'She had mentioned that her family home was in Yokohama, and that her family there would be the beneficiaries of the insurance policy.'

There was another pause for thought.

'Actually, we don't know where she is.'

'But I was told that this is her brother's home . . .'

'Yes it is. But we don't know. As a matter of fact, we would like to know where she is ourselves. If she comes by your place again, please can you let us know?'

She sounded like she meant it.

'I most certainly will,' I said. 'Just to make sure . . . Ms Kizuki was sixty-seven on her last birthday.'

'I think she turns sixty-eight in July. Can she even buy insurance at that age?'

'The premiums do become more expensive.'

'I see.'

'Well, thank you for your time.'

'Hello?' She stopped me from ringing off.

'Yes?'

'Was it her? I mean, did she come to your office herself?'

'Sorry?'

'Did grandma actually visit your office in person?'

'Well, no . . .'

'Was it a woman in her early forties?'

'Yes. She asked for information on the different policies.'

She fell silent again for a moment. 'I mean, you can't conclude a contract without her actually being there at least once, can you?'

'No we can't. Especially since she is rather advanced in years.'

'I'm sure she won't show up. In fact, I think you're probably wasting your time looking for her.'

After the call, I stepped out of the booth and walked in the afternoon sun towards Shinjuku station. It had been a careless lie, pretending to be from an insurance company. And as the woman on the other end of the phone had pointed out, a sixty-seven-year-old woman probably wouldn't be eligible for insurance anyway. The whole telephone incident had served only to add to my suspicions that my mind had been deteriorating since fracturing my thigh.

Actually, deteriorating wasn't the right word. Because if I wanted to, I probably could think very sharply. But there was something that somehow made me not want to. Something deep in my heart that made me refuse to be careful and alert.

I got on an express train on the Odakyu Line, then changed to the local train at Seijogakuenmae station. Kitami station was the next stop. It appeared that Mutsuko's family, or at least the woman I had talked to, had seen the younger Mutsuko. They had been surprised to see her looking about forty-two or forty-three years old and, just like me, they'd suspected that she was a different person. They probably still couldn't believe it was her.

Mutsuko had hidden herself away. Her beauty was a monstrosity in the eyes of people who knew her as a sixty-seven-year-old, and perhaps all she could do to avoid their understandable surprise, doubts and curiosities was simply to disappear. I could imagine the anxieties and solitude of ageing, but I couldn't imagine what life was like for someone who'd become young again. But when I thought of her white nakedness, the feel of her skin, her warmth, her smell and her intensity, I could only imagine that she was losing herself in the pleasures of youth. Such thoughts tortured me as sharp pangs of jealousy, jabbing me every time the train lurched forward.

* * *

'What's going on?' asked my son Shinichi as we sat eating dinner together. 'Mom's always out.'

'You don't like that?'

'It's fine with me.'

'Then it's fine. It's not as if we don't see her.'

'I wouldn't like it if I were you.'

'For a long time, I wasn't around either.'

'Doesn't mean you should let her do whatever she wants.'

'She's increased her magazine's circulation to twenty thousand copies. And they do most of the work with just the three of them. It's not something you can do without being fully committed.'

'You're too understanding. Could even say you were cold.'

'Your mother's good at what she's doing. What is there to gain by getting in her way when she is clearly very committed? Besides, I'd never hear the end of it if I did.'

'Fine, if it's fine with you.'

'I'm fine with it. It's a whole lot better than her staying at home and complaining all the time.'

'It's just that you look . . . desolate.'

'I'm not at all desolate. If you continue to be too sensitive to these things, then when you get married, the disappointment is going to crush you.'

'Not all women are like Mom.'

'Don't be stupid. You rarely find a woman as great as your mother.'

'You really mean that?'

We had decided not to insult each other in front of our children. Of course it was better if my wife was home for dinner, but my wife's thinking was as follows: Babying a husband that had suffered a mental breakdown at work would only make him over-dependent on the wife. The wife's individuality would be compromised, and family life would become unbearable. The best treatment was for the wife to have her own world and not provide the husband with a place to escape to.

She didn't say this to me in person, but this was what was written in an anonymous column in her town magazine, a copy of which had been sent to me at the hospital. I immediately knew that this was how my wife saw my situation and that in a way she was justifying her own decisions. My wife was probably right, though. If she'd stayed at home and treated me like a sick person, I wouldn't be the way I was. I had no intention at all of becoming dependent on someone. Especially after reading a quote about being 'not afraid to be called a bad wife' in that column.

Shinichi went upstairs and I turned on the TV, left feeling alone in my own home as always. 'Mutsuko,' I breathed out in a low voice – something I should be careful not to make a habit of. Imagine if I were to call out her name in front of my wife.

I noticed the comedy group The Drifters, on TV, reminding me it was Saturday.

'Mutsuko.'

Could she be a figment of my imagination?

Surely she couldn't.

'Mutsuko,' I breathed again, unable to resist.

Was I losing my mind? Escaping into a fantasy, depending on a fantasy, called Mutsuko?

Surely not. It simply wasn't possible that my memories, from the flavour of the food and wine at the restaurant to the details of the hotel room, to my experience with Mutsuko, were figments of my imagination. But at the same time, when I thought about Mutsuko's beauty, the way she was attracted to me, and the perfection of my French and that sexual experience, that all seemed unbelievable, too.

As I soaked up the sounds from the television, I felt a sharp anxiety well up inside me and I set out to search for clues. I sought for a trace, any trace, of Mutsuko. I went to my wardrobe, took out the clothes I'd been wearing that day and searched through every single pocket. But I didn't even have the receipt from the restaurant. I'd thrown it out so my wife wouldn't find it. There was nothing. But it couldn't have been an illusion. It was too vivid, it had lasted too many hours, it just couldn't be an illusion. Besides, the Kizukis in Yokohama had seen how Mutsuko had clearly become younger. But really, though, was it clear? Was it really?

'What's the matter?' I suddenly heard my wife's voice as she struggled to conceal her surprise.

'Hi . . . You're home.'

'What are you doing? Going through your suit like that? Is something the matter?'

* * *

May came after two uneventful months. During that time, my confidence weakened and I began to believe that my experience with Mutsuko had been nothing more than the product of my imagination. There were days when I felt a little surer of myself, however, and it was on one of those days that I contacted the Northern Japan branch of our company to get information on the elderly wife that had left the Miyabayashi household. They were quite helpful and confirmed that she had indeed separated from her husband, told me that her current address was unknown and gave me the address of her older brother's family in Yokohama, saying that they would probably know her whereabouts. Plucking up courage, I called the Kizuki family once again in Yokohama, still pretending to be from an insurance company, but they still didn't seem to know where she was. I even considered staying at that hotel room on the eighteenth floor. But that didn't happen, not at 20,000 yen per night. Of course, I would have happily paid so much if I was going to be able to see Mutsuko, but I couldn't pay that kind of money just for memories.

Whenever there was a fine day, it was inevitably followed by a chilly, rainy one. The built-to-order projects department continued in its stagnation, adding another member along the way to bring the total to seven. The new guy was a forty-two-year-old who used to work at the Ushiku office and who'd suddenly insisted on giving up his position six months ago as its deputy director. He'd been diagnosed with depression soon after, and had been on leave of absence ever since.

On his first day our director said to him, 'Some people call us the rehabilitation department, but I don't want you to succumb to such views. In fact, I want you to give a hundred and twenty per cent to any work you are assigned to.'

The new guy responded with a serious expression. 'That kind of encouragement is about the worst thing you can give to someone with depression.' He didn't seem to think this was a strange thing to say and nobody mentioned anything about it. He was simply welcomed without fanfare and he did nothing that seemed particularly strange after that. I think everyone had just given up.

I had given up too, although a passively desperate 'Aah,' would occasionally slip from my mouth. It was an attempt to release the pressure of my mourning and to stem my desire for Mutsuko. Then it happened, one cloudy afternoon in the middle of the month.

'What's this? It doesn't have stamps on it. Looks suspicious to me.'

Yoshiko Takamatsu, who'd gone down to the mailbox, placed the envelope in front of me.

'Feminine handwriting. No name. Must be from the "lovers bank".'

'And how would I have that kind of money?' I said, trying to sound casual, but with a quiver of expectation tainting my voice.

'You've got a guilty look on your face.'

'Don't be stupid,' I responded clumsily.

I wanted to open the envelope as quickly as possible. I knew it was from Mutsuko. I'd never seen her handwriting before, but I was certain this was it.

'Shouldn't you hurry up and open it?'

'I don't think this is any of your business, do you?'

'Look at you, trying to act all nonchalant about it.'

'Okay, okay. It's an invoice from a bar, if you really must

know. But I shouldn't have to say these things out loud,' I said, casually tearing the envelope open. There were two sheets of writing paper inside and I read them.

'I wouldn't have thought an invoice could change your expression like that.'

Yoshiko Takamatsu acted mischievously like this sometimes.

'Director,' I called out. 'Are you going to allow such insolence?' Immediately I noticed that my voice had become a pitch higher, and with a hint of an excited chuckle, too. This was really out of character for me and everyone looked at me. But it was no use; I simply couldn't stop the wave of joy that had suddenly hit me. I laughed again and added, 'And it's not even the end of the month,' in a voice too loud for office hours, before I finally got my excitement under control and put the letter away in my breast pocket.

> *Please accept my apologies for disturbing you.*
> *On the third floor of that hotel – above the second-floor*
> *reception – there is a small coffee shop called Elaine.*
> *I will wait there for an hour from 6:30 today.*
> *If your schedule permits, please come.*
> *Kizuki*

I just couldn't wait for five o'clock to come around! But it was less than ten minutes to that hotel and if I'd rushed over right then, I would have been waiting for over an hour. Nevertheless, I found myself leaving the office at four minutes past five and hurrying straight over. Of course, mainly I was overjoyed to be seeing Mutsuko again. But part of my happiness also stemmed from the knowledge, confirmed by the letter in my hand, that this was in no way an illusion.

Now I held the letter, I felt it had been obvious from the start that this all couldn't have been an illusion. But with such a feeling came a realisation of just how unsure I'd felt at a subconscious level. Then again, wasn't it natural to feel so unsure inside? Especially when considering what had happened – meeting a sixty-seven-year-old woman who'd suddenly and clearly become about forty, with whom I'd then slept. Not doubting myself, now that would have been mad.

Now I had Mutsuko's letter in my jacket breast pocket, I had proof that she existed. As I walked, I placed a hand on the letter. And once I did, I didn't want to let go, so I kept my hand there. I might have looked to passers-by like I was suffering from chest pains. So I forced a frown in an attempt not to smile and pretended to be a worker with a problem on his mind.

I rushed up the escalator to the lobby, passing by an elderly American couple at the top who'd stepped aside when they saw what a hurry I was in.

'Thank you. I'm running late,' I said quickly as I strode out across the lobby.

That's when I realised. I had spoken English. And I had done so pretty much unconsciously, without having to construct a sentence in my mind beforehand. So it was English this time? How suave of her. How incredible. I was already within reach of her mysterious energy.

I ran up the stairs next to the reception desk and walked along the third-floor hallway that looked down over the lobby and was lined with stores selling jewellery, furs and designer clothes. The coffee shop Elaine was located towards the end of the hall.

I was, of course, much too early. In fact, it was only eleven minutes past five. That meant it had taken me just seven minutes to get there. A sure sign that I was getting a little too excited.

'Welcome.'

'I'm supposed to be meeting someone here, but I'm a little early.' I stuck my head in just in case. 'I'll come back later. Excuse me.'

'We look forward to seeing you then'.

I found a bathroom, went in and looked in the mirror – only to find the flushed face of a forty-eight-year-old staring back at me. What a sight. I looked drunk. I needed to calm down. If only I didn't appear so ugly. If only I were a little younger. If only I was forty, at least.

I washed my face, wiped it with a handkerchief, tutted to myself at having wet the collar of my suit, then took a deep breath, telling myself I still had an hour to go. Then I got into a stall, closed the door, took out Mutsuko's letter, unfolded it and read it again. I kissed the place where she had signed her name. Kizuki.

Why hadn't she signed her name Mutsuko? Could this be some kind of plot by the Kizuki family? Surely not. There was no way they could know about what had happened at this hotel. Besides, what would they have to gain from luring me here? Enough of this paranoia, I told myself, and I set off down to the lobby. Then I returned soon enough to the third floor to pass the time window shopping. Why hadn't she made the meeting time six o'clock? Even 5:30 would have been fine with me.

At around 5:40, I went into Elaine and sat there with a coffee in front of me. I was happy to find I'd been wanting her this much and I was exhilarated by the fact that I still had such passion. And that when I thought of her there was not a trace of my cynicism. It had been a long time since I had last been able to see a woman simply as lovable and beautiful. A long time since I'd got past my jaded view of all women as self-centred, fickle, stubborn, unworldly, shallow people. But when it came to Mutsuko, I was intoxicated by her charms and could see her only in a favourable light. I wanted so much to make that feeling last as long as possible, even if it meant blocking my judgement and controlling my sensibilities. Then I saw her standing at the entrance. Watching me.

She had the same hairstyle and was wearing the same outfit as when I had last seen her two months ago. It somehow made me want to protect her. I stood up.

'Welcome,' I heard the coffee-shop staff say.

She smiled and came towards me. 'I came fifteen minutes early, so I could wait for you,' she said, dropping her gaze.

'It's been a while,' I said from the bottom of my heart.

'Yes, it has.' She gave a small nod and sat down across from me.

It wasn't too hot that day, so her kimono didn't look out of place, but I was moved by how she'd selected her outfit of March to wear in May – a time when some of the days can be as warm as midsummer. I felt overwhelmed with a desire to protect her, although from what, I didn't know. I was also relieved that she hadn't become distant from me in the time since we last met.

'I came looking like this intentionally,' she said.

'Intentionally?'

'Because I changed.'

I turned my eyes to her appearance again. The waitress came to take our order, and Mutsuko ordered an iced coffee. After the initial impression made by her choice of clothing began to fade, I noticed she didn't appear to be emaciated or in need of protection at all. In fact, her hair was set neatly and her kimono had been fitted sharply.

'You've lost a little weight,' I said.

'Yes.'

She was even more beautiful than before. And although part of me didn't want to admit it, she was clearly younger. It was unbelievable – although perhaps it should have been very believable to me, having witnessed her previous transformation from an old woman. But now she looked like she was in her thirties, and her early thirties at that. Perhaps she was even in her twenties?

It goes to show just how strongly people's impressions can be coloured by preconceptions. I hadn't noticed it when she'd walked in and sat down in front of me, but now nobody would guess she was in her forties. More likely a young wife of thirty or not quite. All the while she kept her eyes on the table, as if silently enduring my gaze.

'You're younger,' I said.

'I thought you'd be surprised. That's why I came in the same outfit as last time.'

'I see,' my voice cracked. What had happened since I had last seen her? What had she been doing? Anxiety shot through me once again.

'I thought I might never see you again.'

She nodded, keeping her gaze down.

'I missed you.'

A powerful sensation welled up inside me, almost bringing tears to my eyes. I was being overwhelmed by her youth and a sense of defeat began to fill my chest.

'Just like last time,' she said in a low voice. 'I've booked a room.'

'I see.'

Emotions were tangling up inside me and I couldn't tell if I was happy or afraid. I mean, of course I was pleased, but I also had the feeling that this kind of happiness could only come at the price of some misfortune.

'You know the Spanish restaurant in the basement?'

'Was there one?'

'Yes. I went ahead and made a reservation.'

The room this time was on the twenty-fifth floor. There were no high-rises in view from the window and the lights from private homes, street lamps and a stream of cars fanned out low and far into the distance. Down below was a park. There were lamps lighting up sections of the lawn and the benches around the fountain. This was where certain weekly magazines claimed to have secretly taken photos of couples having sex behind the bushes. But on that night there was nobody on the lawn and very few people walking around, which made it seem lonely and sad.

On entering the room, Mutsuko insisted I went ahead and showered first. Then I listened to the sound of water as Mutsuko took a shower too. I thought over the evening's dinner and remembered how she'd said she didn't have the courage to talk about the two months she'd been away. She said she would tell me about it sometime. That not a lot had happened. And that, 'You could say I was asleep.' But surely it wouldn't take courage to talk about being asleep.

'This isn't something I should really say,' she told me.

'Please tell me whatever you want. I want to hear anything you have to say.'

Because her manner of speech hadn't changed, I found myself speaking to her in a polite way. So telling myself that we were closer than that, I made a conscious effort to speak more casually.

'So what is it?'

'It's odd for a sixty-seven-year-old to say this but—'

'Sixty-seven? Anyone can see that you aren't that kind of age.'

'But I am. My memories and the way I feel haven't changed. I can't forget that fact either.'

'And?'

'Well—' She gave a shy smile. It was a perfectly natural shy smile, without a hint of pretence. A smile you never see on the faces of most young women these days. It made me feel like a sweet, warming flame had been lit in my heart.

'I had my period.'

I was shocked. Caught off guard. But then, that had been her way from the beginning. When she'd asked me to talk sex to her, when she'd invited me to the room on the eighteenth floor, this reserved woman sitting in front of me had done so without ever mincing her words.

'Really?'

She had her head down, so I couldn't tell from her expression how she felt about it. But she wasn't smiling. Of course, there was no way she wasn't experiencing something like happiness, but perhaps her fear was stronger than the joy. It reminded me of a scene from a Thomas Mann novel I'd read as a student. Where an old woman delights at the return of her period, only to find the bleeding had been caused by cancer.

But Mutsuko wasn't an old woman, so I pushed such thoughts out of my mind. She was now not much older than thirty, after all, so it was only natural that she would be having periods. I found it adorable how she couldn't help mentioning it and privileged that she had chosen me to share this with. I imagined it must be an experience more touching than any man could ever imagine. But I couldn't even say, 'That's great.'

'What's clear,' I said instead, 'is that you are definitely, unmistakably and miraculously becoming younger.'

'Yes.'

'This is a truly amazing thing. And I hesitate to say it, but if this was ever to reach the news, the whole world would be sent into a frenzy.'

'No.' She shook her head. 'I don't want to even think about it.'

I was warmed, relieved even, by the sudden youthfulness and intimacy of her tone.

'Of course, they would make a fuss about the need for proof.'

'I don't have much time. This is all happening so fast–' she said softly.

'Fast?'

'My arm–' she said, sliding her left hand across the table towards me.

'What is it?'

I looked timidly at the exposed white of her arm.

'Pinch it,' she said, grabbing the skin on her arm with her right hand. 'Go on.' Wanting me to do the same, she moved her left arm in front of me. I reached out my right hand and touched her white skin.

'You can't pinch it, can you?'

I sensed a desperation in her tone.

'I'm young,' she said, as if lamenting the fact.

I tried to pinch her skin with my thumb and index finger, but the youthful tightness of it made it impossible.

'You're right. I can't.'

Perhaps it was her behaviour and gestures making her look older than she was, because when I touched her, I felt she could have been twenty-five, if even that.

'You saw what I looked like at the end of last year,' she said, trying to stay calm. 'Well, it's May now. What's going to happen to me?' she continued softly, with her chest trembling a touch, as if nervously gasping for air.

* * *

Mutsuko stepped out of the bathroom with a towel wrapped around her body. And as she turned to close the door, I was touched by her profile. She was standing very straight, as if braving a tragedy, and it made her seem somehow unapproachable. She looked at me and I felt all erotic feelings crumble away. Then she removed her towel and stood beautiful before me. I sensed sadness in her eyes, which soon sparkled with tears. Then she stretched her arms towards me without moving from the spot, as if there were a fence preventing her from getting any closer. I rushed over and embraced her and she clung to me as if she were drowning. Then I heard and felt her quiet sobs.

The drops on the back of her neck couldn't cling to the firmness of her skin and I caressed her young, taut shoulders. She passionately placed her lips on mine and I knew what was making her so scared. What if she continued to get younger? What if she became a younger woman? Then a young girl?

Then an infant? I didn't have the answer.

'It's silly isn't it?' said Mutsuko. 'For an old woman to be afraid of the future.'

'No, it isn't.'

'To not be able to appreciate my youth.'

'I'm sure you can stay the way you are now.'

'I have to believe that.'

'You're beautiful. Everything about you is sparkling.'

'Look at me,' she said. 'Look at my youth.'

We collapsed onto the bed. Urgently, desperately, I grabbed, caressed, clutched and gently touched her young body. I turned her onto her stomach, then roughly onto her back. All the while kissing, licking and sucking every part of her before making passionate love to her. I got the sense that someone or something was endowing me with strength. Felt I wasn't the only one admiring and greedily drinking in Mutsuko's youth. That the someone or something endowing me with strength was experiencing all these sensations through me. Whatever it was, it didn't feel evil. But it didn't feel divine either. What kind of a god would drive my tongue to taste between her sweet, young thighs?

Perhaps it was my own sense of powerlessness that made me imagine the existence of another. Mutsuko's age reversal was beyond human capability, and my sexual prowess didn't seem like that of a forty-eight-year-old. Having said that, once midnight had passed, all I wanted to do was rest. Maybe my sexual prowess had simply been a case of middle-aged man's enthusiasm for a young woman. Maybe it had been sentimental of me to imagine 'a grand force beyond human capability' earlier.

Mutsuko's hair touched my chin and her cheek rested still

against my chest. Her shoulders moved in time with my breathing and I gently stroked her hair. So black and sleek, with each strand seeming full of life. My hair, in comparison, though thick and wiry in my twenties, was now weak and soft, with grey strands scattered here and there. Mutsuko's hair had been the same as mine, though. So unless this was some sort of clever trick, impossible things were definitely happening to her. That woman with thin, grey hair was here now as someone in her twenties. And even if it were possible to question whether the grey-haired woman and Mutsuko were the same person, the forty-two or forty-three-year-old Mutsuko and the Mutsuko in my arms definitely couldn't be different people. Other than Mutsuko, I was probably the only person who was aware of this.

But was it really right for me to keep this kind of thing secret? Having said that, would it even be possible to tell people and make them believe it? Of course, if Mutsuko continued to grow younger, this miracle could be verified by scientists. But Mutsuko would lose her private life. It could also be possible, as Mutsuko feared, that she might not have long to live. It wasn't impossible that she could become a young girl, then an infant, then a baby, and then finally disappear. And I couldn't bear the thought of exposing that life to science or the curiosities of people in general. Perhaps there were plenty of happenings like this in this world. Maybe things like this do occasionally happen, but people keep them secret to avoid causing mass hysteria. If that were true, then perhaps these things happened more than people thought.

'Tomorrow—' Mutsuko murmured.

'Tomorrow?'

'Can you buy a camera and photograph me?'

'Let's do that. Let me photograph you.'

'Yes.'

'I'm glad.'

'About what?'

'I was worried you would disappear tomorrow morning.'

'I'll be here.'

'I'm glad.'

'Can you come out at five-thirty?'

'I'm not going to work.'

'But you should.'

'No, I don't have to. There's nothing for me there.'

'I'm sleepy.'

'So am I.'

'I don't want to, but I'm going to fall asleep.'

'So am I.'

Next morning, I called home and said I'd been given a proper assignment at work for a change. Then I called my company to tell them that I'd be taking the day off sick. Mutsuko didn't say anything as she saw me lying to my wife and then the company. She just looked away. She seemed like the kind of person who would usually try to stop a man from doing that sort of thing. But at the moment she couldn't afford to do so, so she was putting her own feelings first. I would usually find such a show of self-importance in a woman to be disagreeable, but emotions can be fickle and I found it moving, how she listened to my calls in silence.

Mutsuko ordered room service for breakfast and I felt a slight twinge in my stomach when I thought of the cost. If we stayed another night, I would run out of cash. On top of that, she was asking for a camera. I should somehow be able to pay for that in instalments, but I couldn't afford any more luxuries in the hotel. I could borrow money from a consumer credit company, but I didn't have my wage slip on me, and I probably couldn't get a loan immediately anyway.

'I have money,' Mutsuko said, as if reading my mind. 'Don't worry.'

'I can't let you pay for everything.'

'I'm not saying I have more money than I can spend, but I can at least afford a little luxury for the two of us.'

She told me that her husband had been one of the richer people in the northern town in which they'd lived, and, though she didn't get any money from her divorce, as it had been her decision to leave, she had been saving for a long time in preparation for the day she would go.

'I'm tough when it comes to things like that,' she said with a wry smile. 'But I couldn't stay tough, so I jumped from the platform.'

'The platform of a station?'

She told me how she was immediately rescued and got away with just a fractured vertebra.

'But I really hadn't gotten away with anything.'

'Huh?'

'I mean,' she continued, 'something must have happened then, for me to become like this.'

Hearing the young Mutsuko talk about how she used to be an aged wife from a town in the north, I felt like we'd left everyday life far behind and were now enjoying being in our own insane world. I felt as if a heavy load had been taken off my shoulders, and time passed in peaceful indulgence.

Eventually Mutsuko put on her clothes. Cream-coloured slacks, a white blouse, a yellow summer cardigan and a light green scarf. It was a simple outfit, but I felt like I had come face to face with reality. Youth, for the first time, was standing in front of me in its most fitting form. Taking the pins out one by one, she said, 'I'm afraid this is all I could do with my hair.' I thought how this must be what it was like to come under the spell of a woman. Like it would give me dreamlike happiness to immerse myself in Mutsuko. To drop out of society together.

We went out to the west side of Shinjuku station to buy a camera and I had fun haggling the price down in the crowded store. I felt that today, the city I'd been commuting to had become a different place entirely. Then I put the film in the camera at the store and began taking photos of Mutsuko as soon as we stepped out into the street. I admired her as I captured her with the camera, appreciating the true beauty of her every movement.

We sat down at an outdoor café at the bottom of a high-rise and I took a few more photos of her. Then, even after I'd finished, I allowed my gaze to linger on her.

'Why don't you look at something else?' She shot me a fed-up smile.

'I don't want to look at anything else.'

'People are watching us.'

'I don't care.'

There wasn't much chance that someone from work would be in this area during the day, and I didn't mind if they did see me anyway. I just didn't care. I felt that by immersing myself in Mutsuko, I was enacting revenge on my long career and putting myself on trial.

'There is just one thing I'd like you to fix,' I said.

'What is it?'

'Your manner of speech isn't really suitable for a young woman.'

She dropped her gaze for a moment, then suddenly said, 'Whaddaya want me to do?'

'No, that's going too far.'

'I don't think so. There are plenty of young girls who talk like that. I've even seen a girl referring to herself the way men do, as "*ore*".'

'Well then, I guess you ought to keep it up.'

'I have been aware of this. But you know it's not easy to suddenly change the way you speak. I find myself tempted to say things like, "Would you care to try it on?"'

'You're good.'

'Look, it's already past two. Want to grab a pizza, uncle?'

'Now you're talking like a teenager.'

We both laughed. I felt I could be truly happy if I just believed that I was. Then we walked to the hotel and had pizza at a terrace restaurant.

By the time we got back to the room, the late-afternoon sun was shining through the window. I closed the curtains, thinking that her naked body would come out more beautiful if I took the pictures in the dark using a flash. Mutsuko didn't object and readily slipped off everything she was wearing. She tried to massage off the marks left by her brassiere. I helped her, then placed my lips there. 'You mustn't,' she said, but I couldn't suppress my desire, and the photography was put off until later.

The next morning I woke up to the sound of the phone ringing. It was reception.

'It's eleven o'clock. We would like to inform you that it is check-out time, sir.'

Mutsuko wasn't there.

'The lady requested that we call you to confirm what you would like to do.'

'I'll leave right away. Thanks.'

'You're welcome, sir.'

As expected, she had disappeared. Even though I had checked with her as we were falling asleep.

'You won't leave, right?'

'No.'

'I don't want to wake up to find you aren't here.'

'I won't leave.'

But she had lied. She had left. Struck by a sense of hopelessness, I said out loud, 'She's gone,' in a kind of sob, and collapsed to the floor. I mustered up whatever energy I could and put on my clothes, then looked for the film. At least that was still there.

I'd stuffed so many containers of film in my pockets that they were bulging as I walked down to place the key on the reception desk.

'It looks like I'm thirty minutes late.'

'That's no problem, sir. Thank you very much.'

Again, Mutsuko had already paid for everything. Carrying the camera in my hand, I dragged my feet towards the city under the dazzling May sun.

That night my wife was home. Shinichi was there, too. After the three of us ate dinner together, I stood in the living room looking out at the garden. I could hear my wife doing the dishes. She hadn't said anything about my absence, and when I explained that I'd been working she simply responded encouragingly, 'It's not a bad thing, to do so once in a while.'

A spider's web on the garden light caught my eye. I noticed Shinichi's reflection in the window as he came and stood behind me.

'Dad?' he said quietly. 'I saw you in Shinjuku yesterday.'

4

'Does your mother know?' I asked my son discreetly.

'Well, of course I didn't tell her,' he replied, equally discreet. He stood about two fists taller than me. I could hear the sound of running water from the kitchen.

'Let's go to your room.'

'All right.'

Shinichi headed for the stairs. As I tried to follow him, I heard my wife say, 'There's ice cream,' followed by the sound of dishes being placed on the dish rack.

'I'm fine for now, thanks. I'm just going up to Shinichi's room for a bit.'

'To do what?'

'Listen to some records.'

'How unusual.'

I carried on upstairs and walked in the door that Shinichi had left open, suddenly realising just how unusual this was. Like the first visit to a friend I hadn't seen in a while; the basics were the same, but many things were unfamiliar. This was partly because I had lived away from home for a long time, but also because Shinichi preferred to keep his room private.

'Take a seat on the bed,' he said, turning round the chair in front of his desk and sitting down.

'Do you really want to listen?' he said.

'To what?' I replied, gazing out of the window.

'A record.'

'Oh, no.'

'Wouldn't it be suspicious if she can't hear music?'

'I guess so. Can you put one on then?'

'What do you want to listen to?'

'I don't know well enough to choose.'

Shinichi stood up, switched on his stereo and began flicking through his records. I was a little relieved. I was expecting him to be angry at me. After all, he had just caught his own father messing about with a young woman. Surely he was disappointed in me. Or maybe he was already beyond disappointment. A child who'd already watched his spineless father suffer from a mental breakdown as soon as he'd made deputy director of sales. He probably didn't see me as someone he needed to surpass. The sound of the needle on the record interrupted my train of thought, then a loud guitar chord followed.

'It's a bit loud.'

'There's no point if it's not loud.'

'Meaning?'

'Meaning it doesn't sound good.'

'Well we didn't come here to listen to records.'

'But it sounds great, though, doesn't it?'

'Huh?'

'It sounds great, doesn't it?'

'Yes, it does.'

'Why don't you sit down?'

'All right. It's just that I haven't looked out of this window in a while. The view is refreshing.'

'Wait for it.' He stuck his palm out towards me as if to stop my words. 'Coming up now . . . after this part,' he said, pointing to the speakers. The guitar shifted rhythm, then continued on. I was a little taken aback. Shinichi really had wanted me to listen to his records. Me, of all people. It was hard to believe. My son wanted to empathise with me. He wanted me to listen to what he thought was good music. This possibility hadn't occurred to me at all and, unable to respond, I stood frozen in place, staring out at the empty, three-metre-wide suburban street beyond the window.

I was surprised that my son, my third-year college-student son, would want to listen to music with his dad. But inside he was still a child and I felt something like love for him well up inside me. I turned towards him slowly. Shinichi reached for the dial on the stereo and lowered the volume.

'The rest is nothing special,' he said.

'I see.'

'Why don't you sit down?'

'Okay.'

I finally sat down on the bed, feeling like we'd been dodging the subject at hand.

'I'm sorry, but I saw you two get into the hotel lift together.'

'From where.'

'Next to the reception. By the–'

'No. I mean, where did you first notice me?'

'At Yodobashi Camera.'

That meant that he had seen almost everything. All my shameless flaunting of Mutsuko. My carefree display of infatuation.

'You must have been watching us for a couple of hours.'

'I don't think so. At least, it didn't feel that long.'

'Right.'

'I was busy thinking about other things, like whether I should say hi and stuff.'

Despite what he'd seen, he still had the composure and decency not to launch immediately into a criticism of me, even playing me some music first. Could it be that he was no longer a child after all? That he'd instead become so much of an adult that his father now looked pathetic to him? Then again, he'd followed us for close to two hours. Surely that was a sign of youth. Somewhere inside me, I actually felt a glimmer of happiness at the realisation that my son had been taking such an interest in me. But still I had no real idea of what he was feeling or thinking.

'What you told us,' said Shinichi. 'About getting a decent assignment at work for a change. It isn't true, is it?'

'No, it isn't.'

I didn't like having to admit such a thing to my son, but there was nothing else I could do.

'So what is she? That woman.'

'Well . . .'

'Is she your woman, Dad?'

'I guess so.'

'She mustn't know.'

'Know what?'

'Know you, Dad.' He dropped his gaze.

'I see.'

'I was surprised how pretty she was. And young.'

'Yeah.'

I repressed the urge to revel in the compliment.

'For that kind of person to be seduced—'

'I didn't seduce her.'

'I just don't know that side of you.'

'It's not like this is something I do all the time, you know.'

'I wonder what she's attracted to in you?'

'How would I know?'

'Well, I come from you. Which means I've inherited at least something from you. So when I saw something unexpected like that, I began to think there might be something in me that I myself haven't realised yet – watching you and thinking those kinds of things, it didn't feel like two hours had passed at all.'

It suddenly occurred to me that I might be able to fabricate a story. Tell him that I wasn't sleeping with Mutsuko. That it was what is known as industrial espionage. Although at the same time, I found myself wanting to boast to my son of how I'd won the heart of a beautiful woman.

'Is that Nikon yours?'

'Huh?'

'The camera.'

'Yes, it is.'

Actually, Mutsuko had paid for it, but I had it now and at that moment I didn't want to admit that it belonged to her.

'Can I use it?'

'Sure.'

Still I couldn't make up my mind whether he was still a child or whether he'd become an adult. Perhaps he was at a difficult age in between.

Suddenly he turned round and opened his desk drawer, making me wonder what he was going to show me.

'Basically, what I want to say is . . .' His hand reached into the drawer but came out with nothing more than a nail clipper.

'It's not so smart to be carrying on like that in Shinjuku where anyone could see you.'

'I know.'

'Because if you keep doing that, Mom's going to find out.'

'Yeah. You're right'

'That's all I wanted to say. You can go now.'

He picked up an FM radio guide off the floor, placed it on his desk and began cutting his nails with his back to me. The guitar music was still playing quietly in the background.

You can go now, huh? He really turned the tables on me then. But this isn't just the hopeless affair of an over-the-hill father. It's a truly incredible experience. I so much wanted to tell him all about this and make him understand. But there was no way I could ever make him believe or prove it. The closest thing I had to proof was the film, but that meant nothing to someone who hadn't seen the Mutsuko of the past. So I simply stood up, took a glance at Shinichi's back, walked out and closed the door behind me.

The film. I thought about the film. As for the photos I'd taken outside, I could get those developed anywhere. But the photos I'd taken in the room, they were much more intimate. I'd photographed her naked young body in detail. Her toned shoulders. The peach fuzz on her arms. I'd drunk in the faint odour of her armpits. Captured the single mole on her smooth back. Recorded her milk-white buttocks. The mark left on one by the grip of my hand. Noted the redness of it and the speed with which it faded away. I recalled the unexpected weight and softness of her breasts when I laid her on her back, the soft blush of her nipples and the way they reacted to my touch. Her delicate navel. The glorious contrast between her porcelain-white skin and her jet-black pubic hair that was neither thick nor thin. I'd guided her legs apart to explore her sex. Its youth. Its colour. Its pulse. I'd placed my head between her thighs. Feeling their fullness, feeling their warmth and shutting myself off entirely from the world outside.

A sudden desire fired up inside me and brought me to a standstill halfway down the stairs. Was it okay to feel like this so soon after talking to my child? Did this mean I was feeling less like a father? Or remind me that I'd never really felt like a father at all?

'Something the matter?' asked my wife, looking up at me.

'Huh?'

'I heard your footsteps stop and wondered what had happened.'

'I'm okay,' I said with a little too much feeling, hinting at the after-effects of my mental breakdown.

I went into the kitchen, sat down and ate ice cream.

'To be honest,' I said, 'it's not true that I've become busier at work.'

'Yes?'

She was sitting across from me reading the evening paper and eating ice cream.

'I stayed in a hotel by myself and I bought an expensive camera, too. I was in the mood to do something crazy like that.'

'I wouldn't call that crazy.'

'Right.'

'Did you have enough money?'

'Just enough.'

'It's all right if you splurge 20, 30,000 yen once in a while.'

'I suppose so.'

And that was the end of her inquiry. A simple exchange of words that came quickly to a close as she flipped to the next page of the newspaper. Was she showing consideration to the ill? Or was she simply not interested? I had no idea what I may have just started and as I continued to eat my ice cream I couldn't help but feel that, whatever it was, this couldn't be the end of it. Something between us was unresolved.

* * *

On Sunday I walked around Yokohama. I had no idea where to find Mutsuko, but I felt that I would at least be closer to her than if I'd stayed at home. The Kizuki family home was located in an old residential area on the mountain side of Tanmachi station on the Toyoko Line. It was a two-storey house built on a plot of about 230 square metres surrounded by a concrete brick wall. To the east of the house was a four-metre-wide street. The front entrance faced south-east and the general wooden structure of the house was about twenty years old. The front entrance did seem as if it had been newly extended, however, and other renovations included new sashes in the first-floor windows and the addition of an extra room on the north side. I got the impression that it was a house that was well looked after. Considering that I worked at a construction company, I probably should have felt that such a house be demolished and replaced with a prefabricated one, but such thoughts were in the past for me now.

I buzzed the intercom and a middle-aged woman answered. 'Yes?'

'Hello. I'm from Tokyo House Construction. We're conducting a survey on extensions and renovations.'

'I'm sorry, but I'm in the middle of something,' she said, and cut me off. I pressed the button again.

'I told you I was busy,' said the woman, clearly annoyed.

'I'm sorry, but can I just ask one brief question? Do you have an elderly person living with you?'

'No, we don't.' I was cut off again.

Mutsuko's sister-in-law was an old woman, and as far as I knew she was living with them, but I could understand why she might not tell the truth. But it didn't really matter. Mutsuko wasn't an old woman anyway, so the question was meaningless.

There was no way Mutsuko would be there, I thought, and I began walking down the gentle hill towards Tanmachi station. It did occur to me that perhaps what I should have been doing at that moment was to try and to pull myself together instead. To try and regain my professional competence and motivation. But then again, there was probably no way I could shake my questionable reputation before retirement. And even if I could, what would it mean?

But before the balloons.

A strange voice spoke in my mind. Balloons? What are you talking about?

Are you sure we can move freely in Space? Right and left we can go, backward and forward freely enough, and men always have done so. I admit we move freely in two dimensions. But how about up and down? Gravitation limits us there.

I recognised the words. They were from a book by H. G. Wells that I hadn't read since I'd been at school. *The Time Machine.* That's where the words were from.

Man can go up against gravitation in a balloon, and why should he not hope that ultimately he may be able to stop or accelerate his drift along the Time-Dimension, or even turn about and travel the other way?

I stopped in my tracks and turned round. There were no people walking or cars driving down the street and these words that had remained long forgotten, yet returned so vividly, made me feel Mutsuko must be somewhere nearby. But there was no one around. Not a man, not a woman, not a cat or a dog. So I continued down the sloping path on the side of the street that wasn't draped in shadow.

When I had been with Mutsuko, I had been able to speak French, although there had been some words I wasn't able to understand. Maybe she'd enabled me to retrieve anything that had ever been in my memory. So I wasn't endowed with an entirely new ability but reacquainted with a long-forgotten one instead.

Then again, it couldn't really be caused by Mutsuko, as strange things had begun to happen before I had even met her. At least the premonition about the train accident had, anyway. We'd been on opposite ends of the ward at that time, but we hadn't actually met. Could it be that we had both come under the influence of some great, invisible force – one which had had an even stronger effect on Mutsuko? Maybe it was this force that was enabling me to recall Wells, and maybe this meant that Mutsuko wasn't necessarily nearby. I walked down the hill towards the station, turning round several times along the way. But I didn't come across Mutsuko.

That day, I felt Mutsuko's presence on two more occasions,

caused by the reading of newspaper articles both times. The first was in a paper I'd picked up at Yamashita Park in Yokohama. I never usually pick up discarded newspapers, but this one came flying towards the bench I was sitting at and got tangled round my legs. I felt something radiating from the paper (sorry to put it in a way that sounds, well . . . paranormal, but I don't know how else to put it) and I picked it up.

From the Kyodo News Service in the Yomiuri Shimbun.

Shandong Province, Yanggu County: Veterinary Hospital Director Wang Tzu-Hsien (64) aged rapidly between his mid forties and mid fifties, losing his two front teeth, his hair turning grey and his eyesight deteriorating to the point that he could no longer read without eyeglasses. But as soon as he turned fifty-eight, his hair turned black again, he grew two new front teeth, his eyesight recovered and his mobility and memory returned to that of someone in his twenties. No scientific explanation for this phenomenon has yet been offered.

Then there was the article in the *Asahi Shimbun* that I picked up from the rack on the train back to Tokyo.

Professor S. Hawking of Cambridge University, England – renowned for his theories on black holes – explained at a Kyoto University lecture organised by the Institute of Theoretical Physics that, 'If the universe, which is currently expanding, reaches its contraction stage, the flow of time will be reversed.'

* * *

This lecture, entitled 'The Arrow of Time', began with footage of a coffee cup breaking, then coming back together as the film is run in reverse. This smashing of the cup illustrated the tendency for time to move from a state of order to disorder, thereby alluding to the second law of thermodynamics. The professor claimed that this thermodynamic arrow of time is pointing in its current direction as the universe has been expanding since the Big Bang. He then went on to state that there is no guarantee that this will continue to be the case in the future. Professor Hawking then said that, if we presume that the universe and time are closed four-dimensionally, then 'If the universe begins to recollapse, the thermodynamic direction of time will be reversed, and head from disorder to order.'

It could, of course, be the case that there was nothing magical at all about my encounter with the two articles. I might have simply felt that way owing to the youthful energy that was flowing within me that made everything appear linked to one special woman. I began to analyse my life. Was I doing any real work? No. But so what? I had a son at university. Again, so what? It wasn't as if I had an unbearable wife. But so what? And I didn't go home for dinner. So what? Wanting to escape the trappings of my middle-aged life, I allowed myself to regress. So what if I chose to walk the streets at night in search of Mutsuko?

Confirming that she wasn't in one part of town, I'd wonder if she might be found in an alleyway somewhere else. Then, after checking there in vain, I'd be sure I might find her if I'd only search the next street along. In this way I kept checking and checking, following unlimited mirages in my mind. And as I did so, I began to give up, waking up to the reality as I walked sober past the drunkards of the night. Out of nowhere, a Baudelaire quote came to mind:

They get drunk so that they don't have their bodies changed to beasts.

I recognised myself partially becoming a beast without alcohol and, enjoying this change in me, I walked the streets until midnight.

On the way to work the next day, another Baudelaire quote sprang to mind.

The filthy metropolis.

It was a line I recognised from a poetry anthology I hadn't read since my university years.

I was reminded of something my boss had said to me.

'I'm not saying this because I'm the director of the rehabilitation department, but to show symptoms of maladaptation is, in a sense, and by sense I mean the natural way for humans to be . . . What I'm saying is that in that sense it can be taken as a healthy reaction. You could even say that there is a lot more wrong with guys who rapidly adapt to one streamlining initiative after another adopted by the company and improve their performance. They may be the ones without emotions, personalities, opinions, or desires. But saying these things isn't going to convince the company to raise your salary. As long as you are working at the company, in the end all you can do to regain your manhood is to become someone who is useful to the company. There's nothing to be gained by running away from this. What's the matter? You're not yourself these days. You're the deputy director. You have to take the responsibilities that come with that more seriously. I can only do so much to cover for you.'

* * *

I can't quite explain why I stopped by Shibuya on the way home. I'd been experiencing one premonition after another since the previous day, so I could no longer be sure if I was acting on one or not. I simply felt guided by something and allowed myself to go along with buying a ticket, boarding a train, then heading over there.

I stepped out of the station and headed for the busy crossing and suddenly there she was. Mutsuko walked passed me, heading to my right. A pulse of joy shot through me before I could properly even register what I'd seen, then I turned and watched her as she strode away under the railway bridge. Emerging from under the bridge, she scurried past the crowds towards Miyamasuzaka and, needless to say, I chased after her. As I followed, part of me was surprised to be thinking that this woman in front of me was Mutsuko. After all, her hairstyle was different and she was wearing a white jacket that was too wide for her at the shoulders. She also had on a red shirt that hung loose from the jacket, baggy trousers and flat, yellow shoes. The red belt of a handbag hung from her shoulder. And the moment she'd flitted past me, I'd noticed she was wearing heavy make-up. She was even walking differently from the Mutsuko of three days earlier – moving briskly ahead with long, confident strides.

The traffic lights were about to turn red and Mutsuko began to run. So I ran too. But when she'd reached the other side of the crossing, she didn't slow back down to a walk. It was like she was running away. Like she was running from me. Could she really be running from me? I had to know, so I caught up with her and called her name softly.

'Mutsuko.'

Without answering, she made a sharp left turn into a street that was barely wide enough for two cars to pass each other. I noticed her back sway as she swiftly turned another corner onto a sloping street too narrow for even a single car. Then she stopped and turned round.

It was Mutsuko all right. But I was amazed by the way she'd changed. It was nothing, of course, compared to her change from an old woman, but a change made more dramatic by heavy use of make-up. She still looked like she was in her mid twenties. But unlike last time, her eyes appeared sharper, as if she were reproaching me for something.

'It looks like I upset you by chasing after you,' I said, trying in vain to stop my voice quaking.

She dropped her gaze and said, 'Come.' Then she turned round and took a few steps up the hill before climbing three small stone steps on the left and opening the battered steel door of an old building. I followed her down a narrow hallway, then up a staircase of similar dimensions. I looked at the movement in her baggy blue trousers as she climbed before my eyes. Watched the sway of her hips. But this time no feelings of desire arose. As she neared the top of a flight of stairs, she unzipped her red handbag and I saw her take out a key. Then, when we reached the fourth floor, she put the key in a door. I stopped in the middle of the staircase and looked up to see her angry profile, and I felt scared that this might be the end. She opened the door and looked at me. 'Come in.'

I quickly followed after her, worried that she might disappear – finding her standing by the window at the end of the room with her back to me, though the only view from the window was a dirty concrete wall. I closed the door.

Immediately to my right-hand side was a gas cooker and a sink, both of which looked as if they'd hardly been used. And in the adjacent room where Mutsuko was standing, I could see the simple concrete shell of the building, with only worn-out tiles to cover thirty or so square metres of floor. In the middle of the floor was a leather sofa that had definitely seen better days. There was also a queen-size bed, which seemed to be the only new thing in the place. Nothing was on the bed except for a light brown, crumpled-up blanket. On the floor were a few containers holding clothing and five or six cardboard boxes. Mutsuko was standing still with her back to me.

'I won't ask any questions if you don't want me to,' I said.

She remained still, unreactive.

'I'm glad I was able to see you again.'

I stood still, making a point not to approach her. Afraid she might start shouting at me at any moment. I noticed her shoulder drop ever so slightly.

'I don't have time.'

It was the familiar voice of Mutsuko. Her gentle voice giving the impression that she was choosing her words. It's all right, I thought. You don't have to try and speak like a young person. You can talk to me in your natural, sixty-seven-year-old way. But perhaps, as young as she was now, that manner of speech no longer felt natural to her.

'I guess I became impatient. Wanting to experience all kinds of things in life. There are so many things I've never done in all my sixty-seven years and now I have such a short time to experience all I can. No matter what I'm doing, I worry that I should be doing something better, more important. Because I really don't have much time at all.'

I looked at her small back in that baggy jacket and felt it a touching sight.

'What makes you say you don't have time?'

'Do you think I do?' she asked, turning to face me.

Her outfit was very unusual, even by the standards of the young women walking around Shibuya. In the first place, young women these days probably didn't wear so much make-up. But having said that, her white foundation and deep red lipstick made her look beautiful. They just didn't match the maturity you could still sense in her eyes.

'I think you do,' I said. 'You're young.'

I could see anger appear in her eyes.

'You're the only one who knows my situation. You're the only person who can understand how I'm feeling. And you say I'm young. How can you give me such a blind response?'

'What do you expect me to say? I've only spent one day with you in March, then another two days and nights more recently.'

'But you know that I'm really a sixty-seven-year-old woman.'

She walked over to the bed and sat down, stood up sharply, then threw herself onto the sofa, face down.

'In just a short time,' I said to her back, 'I've seen you become younger so fast. But all I have is an idea of your fear. I just don't understand enough to know what to think or feel.'

'You don't understand! Well, three days to you is three years to me. Three days and two nights to you means more than three years for me.'

I knelt down on the floor next to where she was lying and gently placed a hand on her back.

'I want to know what happened.' I felt the familiar warmth of her body under my hand. 'And what you're doing alone in a room like this.'

'After I left that hospital, I went back to my husband, pressed my seal on the divorce papers, packed my things and flew to Haneda.' She said all this in one hurried breath and then fell silent again.

'Do you have children?'

'I have two.'

'It hadn't occurred to me.'

'A forty-five-year-old daughter and forty-three-year-old son. How do you think they'd react if they could see me now?'

'Were you living together?'

'No. They both have their own families to occupy their minds. It's not surprising that they left home. My husband didn't trust them. He said his fortune would be lost if he left it to them. Even now that he's in his seventies, he refuses to think about any kind of inheritance. Business is the only thing he can think about.'

'I thought you said he wasn't involved in business. That he was a landowner.'

'He is. Stocks, construction, demolition, rentals, car parks. All he ever did was stare at a portfolio of assets, then go around trying to grab another yen wherever he could.'

Because Mutsuko was young, she reminded me of a school-girl acting the part of an old woman. It brought back memories from when I was a student.

'So you arrived in Haneda and went to your brother's place in Yokohama?'

'No. I didn't want to impose. I stayed at a hotel, looked for an apartment to rent, found one in Honmoku, dropped my things there, then went to see them three or four days later. When they heard that I had separated from my husband, they had grave expressions on their faces, probably worried that they might have to take care of me or pay for my funeral. I remember trying to tell myself that I don't need anyone to take care of me, but realistically I was old, so I couldn't afford to be so sure of myself.'

'I see.'

'I bought this bed when I was at that apartment,' she said, glancing towards it. 'I just bought the bare minimum. A kettle, a pot and a gas stove. Then I asked myself how I would live from then on. I had just about enough money to get by, but I wondered how I could spend my old age in a way that would leave me with no regrets.'

'I see—'

'One night, I suddenly started to feel unwell. My entire body felt heavy and uncomfortable. I wanted to scratch everywhere. I opened my mouth wide, crawled around the room with my mouth still wide open and tried not to make a sound so as not to disturb the neighbours. I was pretty sure I was about to die and was consumed by regret about how I'd wasted my life. Trying to feel something physical, I pinched myself hard all over and the tears came flooding from my eyes.'

I rubbed her back with my hand, not quite sure if I was comforting an old woman or consoling a girl.

'I lost consciousness and, when I came to, two weeks had passed.'

'Two weeks? The way you were? Without anyone finding you?'

'Yes.'

'Without eating anything? Just lying there the way you were when you lost consciousness.'

'When I came to, I wasn't aware that two weeks had passed. It was daybreak, and I just thought that it was the next morning.'

'I see.'

'My body wouldn't move and I was aching all over. I thought that all I could do was to call an ambulance and stay in hospital.'

'I see.'

'But I didn't have a phone because I hadn't thought I would need one. I was going to stand up, go down to the bottom of the building and use the phone or catch a cab. I didn't want to inconvenience anyone else, you see.'

'I see.'

'But I couldn't stand up. I was suffering from exhaustion. I simply couldn't move.'

'Well, I'm not surprised, if you were on the floor for two weeks.'

'I was on my back, looking up at the ceiling and thinking, oh what a sad life it has been. Knowing I'd wasted my life and recognising that part of the blame lay with me, I placed a hand on my chest. And that's when I realised that I had breasts. I mean, that they were no longer flat. I was in my pyjamas at the time and I slid my hand up under them to find them surprisingly full and firm. Then I realised that my whole body felt bloated and suddenly worried in an instant that I might have caught some strange disease, involuntarily crying out "Aargh", kind of like you do.'

'You'd become younger.'

'Well, it took me quite a while to realise it. I wasn't hungry.

Just tired and unable to get up. I remained like that for two days and I still find it all very strange when I think about it now . . .'

'Two days?'

'Well, you see, I wasn't uncomfortable if I just stayed lying down. The only problem was that I couldn't get up. I think God had perhaps done that on purpose so that I wouldn't be too surprised to suddenly see myself younger.'

'But you could see your body.'

'That's right. When I looked at my hands, there were surprisingly young. They were plump, not bony, and all my old blotches were gone. My breasts were big and white. And when I touched my hair, which had been thinning, I noticed it was thicker. I brushed my hair over my eyes and found that it was black. At that moment, I thought I'd either gone mad or had died. That I was in another world.'

'When did you first look into a mirror?'

'Well . . . I suddenly became very hungry, and I could feel strength returning to every part of my body. Isn't that strange? To regain strength by becoming hungry.'

'It's already a pretty strange story. Nothing can surprise me any more.'

'And I knew I didn't have a hand mirror. Just a small mirror on my powder compact. So when I got up, the first thing I did before anything else was to grab my handbag, pour out its contents and look into the small round mirror.'

'And you were about forty-two or -three.'

'I couldn't tell how old I was. Even now, I feel like I could be both about thirty or twenty-two, -three. I might actually even be flitting between those ages.'

'Were you glad?'

'I don't know how many days it took to feel that way. I was afraid. I was hungry and wanted to go outside, but I was afraid to do so. I wanted to look at myself more carefully in the mirror, but I was afraid to do that too. Another couple of days later, I finally calmed down, accepted what had happened to me and went to the Kizuki home in Yokohama. I called them beforehand so as not to surprise them. I told them I would be going over that night and that they shouldn't be alarmed. But the warning didn't really help. Everyone except the children, including my sister-in-law and nephew, had known me when I was in my forties, so you can imagine their surprise. My sister-in-law started feeling unwell and collapsed to her knees the moment she saw me at the front entrance. My nephew didn't think it was me, and he let me into the house, saying that he could "clearly tell from your face that you are related to my aunt" and he would "listen to my situation", but in the end he got all confused, and I was asked to leave.'

'They didn't believe you?'

'It's no surprise. To become ready to believe something like this, you would have to give up on life at least once.'

'Are you referring to me?'

'Yes.'

She looked at me for the first time and smiled. Then pushing herself up, she kissed me on my lips and I felt a trace of lipstick linger there.

'The first night I was at the hotel with you, I began to feel that same sluggishness. An indescribable dullness began welling up around my chest.'

'I can't quite understand the feeling of dullness in the chest.'

'Well, that's the only way I can describe it. I knew that feeling right away. When I thought back to the first time it had happened, I remembered that my chest had been heavy for about two to three days before. I sneaked out of the room and went back to Yokohama by taxi.'

'You said you were living in Tokyo.'

'I was just being cautious. The next night I was hit by another strong wave of this. And once again, I squirmed around with my mouth open. My body felt extremely heavy, like every muscle in my body was rotting, and it made me want to stab a knife into myself just for distraction. It lasted for two, three hours, before it reached a point where I couldn't take it any more. That's when I lost consciousness.'

'For another two weeks?'

'For more than twenty days. Twenty-two to be exact.'

'And you didn't become emaciated?'

'I had just become younger. And before I knew it, I was this age. But how much longer can I stay this way? My last phase lasted from the end of January until the eighth of March. This phase started at the beginning of April and it's the seventeenth of May today. It could come at any moment. The sluggishness will hit me once more and I'll lose consciousness again–'

'But it might not. You might be able to remain the way you are now for ever.'

'A sixty-seven-year-old woman stay this way for ever? Do you really think people get that lucky?'

'There are plenty of episodes of people getting lucky like that. Take me, for instance. An unremarkable middle-aged man who had his way with a beautiful young woman like you.'

'I'm afraid.' She placed her head against my neck. 'I don't like it,' she said, pressing her lips against me repeatedly. I held her tight to calm her down and felt her soft sobbing.

I had no intention of telling her, but I was a little hurt. Mutsuko had been this young since early April, but she had only come to see me almost ten days into May. And even then she'd disappeared after just two days. I had hoped that I meant more to her than that. After all, she had said that I was all she had. So what had she been doing all that time? Setting out to experience all things in life? Trying to gain so many experiences in such a short time? I'm sure that was exactly what she had been doing. But if she were to become younger again, I hoped that she would come and see me before a month had passed.

As soon as this thought passed through my mind, it suddenly hit me. I didn't believe she'd be able to remain the way she was. Human beings tend to want to ascribe rules and find patterns for everything. She'd become a woman in her forties. Then one in her twenties. So next time she should be in her teens or younger. That kind of thing. But if reality followed rules like that, then she wouldn't be this young now. Realising how foolish I'd been to make such assumptions myself, I saw how small and insignificant I really was.

'It's a bit bare, this room,' I said, wanting to change my mood.

'Well, I wanted to live in Tokyo.'

'But even so.'

'Because all the other spaces in the building are offices, there's nobody around at night. So if I have to let out a cry, there will be no one to get suspicious.'

'Let out a cry?'

'You know. When that sluggishness overtakes me. I'm sure I must let out the most terrible cries.'

'But surely if that was the case, your neighbours at the apartment in Yokohama wouldn't have left you alone for two weeks and twenty-odd days.'

'No, I was holding back my cries then, even up to the point where I lost consciousness. Here it's not a problem to cry out.'

'You could maybe cry out for other reasons too . . .'

'Don't be silly. No. Let me go. I must look terrible. After all this crying.'

'I love the dishevelled face of a beautiful woman.'

'What's that supposed to mean?'

'I guess it means I like beautiful women when they aren't consumed with beauty.'

'Well, I'm not a beautiful woman.'

'Actually, I've done a thorough investigation and I must let you know that it's official – you really are a beautiful woman.'

I pushed her down onto the sofa and did exactly as I desired.

Afterwards, Mutsuko showed me something unexpected. She opened a cardboard box, which she was using as a wardrobe, that had underwear stacked neatly inside. That wasn't what was unexpected, though. What was unexpected was when she reached her hand down between the garments and pulled out a navy, velvet package. It was about the size of a large lunch box and a thick rubber band was wrapped around it in a cross.

'What do you think it is?' She gave me a teasing smile.

'I suppose it's not just a block.'

'No.'

'A Rorschach test?'

She sniggered.

'Uncut diamonds?'

'Of course not.'

'A royal jelly drink, or ginseng?'

'Come on, you're being silly.'

'A box with your umbilical cord in it? No, really. I'm not being silly. There was one at home, although it wasn't that big. No, you know what – I give up. There's nothing in my life that I need to wrap in velvet and stash among my underwear, so I'm afraid I can't even begin to imagine what it might be.'

She took off the rubber band without saying a word, then unfolded the cloth to reveal a small pistol.

'It's real,' she said.

'I'm surprised,' I said. And I really was.

'I bought it.'

'Why? No, where? How?'

I tend to assume other people think more or less along the same lines as me usually, so when I imagined Mutsuko buying a gun I was shockingly reminded of the sheer gulf between one person and another.

'I guess it's what you call a Beretta,' I offered.

'It's a Colt Pocket Automatic.'

The words didn't suit her.

'Is that so?'

'It's not that I know a lot about it. I was told when I bought it. Apparently it's a Model M.'

'Where did you buy it?'

'In Yokosuka.'

'From a foreigner?'

'I was approached.'

'Why?'

'I went to this scary-looking place.'

'You slept with a foreigner, didn't you?'

I could feel my gaze turn stern. I suddenly felt a pang of jealousy.

'No, I didn't.'

'But why would someone try to sell a gun to a woman unless he had something going with her? Look, I know I don't have the right to say who you can and can't sleep with. But Yokosuka?'

'I've always wanted to go there. My father was in the navy and he'd worked in Yokosuka for a long time. I hadn't been there since I went there for the Navy Day celebrations as a small child, so I went there on a whim. I'm sure the port has changed a lot, but it felt really familiar. So did the smell of the sea. After that, I thought I'd try to go somewhere a little scary.'

'By yourself?'

'Of course by myself.'

'But why "of course"?'

'That's just how it was.'

'But why would you want to go to a scary place all by yourself?'

'I just wanted to. Of course, I felt scared, but I wasn't a young girl and bad things don't happen so commonly, so I walked into a bar. It was almost empty and it was dark and dirty, but it wasn't scary at all. There was one black man and he smiled at me and we had a beer together.'

'That's enough.'

'It isn't. He said he wasn't a soldier. That he was a sailor. He asked me to go to a hotel with him. I told him I had no intention of doing that, and he just nodded, and that was all. It was like he asked just to be polite. Then we had a second beer together. He'd bought the first round, so I bought the second.'

'Did he bring up the pistol?'

'No, actually it was me. I meant it as a joke. Just because it was that kind of atmosphere. I asked him if he had a pistol. He didn't answer, but his eyes were smiling. Then when I left the bar, he followed me out and asked me to go into an alley with him. When I refused, he whispered that he wanted to sell me a gun.'

'In English?'

'Well, I can understand that much.'

Of course a young woman would, but I was thinking that Mutsuko was sixty-seven years old.

'He gave me a price of 100,000 yen, so I said no way and he reduced it to 80,000 then 60,000. I thought it would be nice to own a gun for 60,000 yen.'

'How about bullets?'

'I have some.'

She skilfully slid out the magazine, showed it to me, then snapped it back in.

'That's all there is to it,' she let out a wry laugh. 'Nothing dramatic happened.'

'And you weren't followed?'

'From Yokosuka? Of course not.'

'I guess it's okay if you just want to keep it.'

'But I want to use it.'

'Don't be stupid.'

'I do, I want to shoot it. I want to blast away my worries. Want to really *do* something. Will you join me?'

'In what?'

'Armed robbery and extortion.'

I let out a laugh of disbelief.

'I'm not joking.' She glared at me and her voice suddenly

turned serious. 'I want to do it, even if I have to do it on my own.'

'Why?'

'Because I want to. Because I don't know when that sluggish-ness will hit me again.'

Her voice quivered. 'It'll be fun. Scaring someone who looks strong. Don't you want to do it? You would if you could, wouldn't you?'

'I don't mean to change the subject, but do you want to get some dinner.'

'I do.'

Was Mutsuko testing my worth as a man?

* * *

After eating out, we returned to the apartment. I picked up the Colt Pocket Automatic Model M for the first time and it sent a shiver down my spine. Just possessing it was a crime, which could lead to arrest and even a custodial sentence. Like a lump of dry ice in my hand, I couldn't wait to put it down. But at the same time, I didn't want her to see me drop it too quickly. Nevertheless, I held on to it for less than twenty seconds before putting it back down on the bed.

'Simply put,' I said, 'armed robbery is a dull idea.'

Mutsuko was trying to balance a glass, a teacup and a bottle of whisky on the cardboard box in front of the sofa. But the top of the cardboard box was less than sturdy, and the teacup and glass looked as if they might tip over at any moment. Mutsuko was trying to flatten the surface by hitting the cardboard box.

'Are you listening?' I asked.

'I'm listening.'

Her response sounded very mature, but her actions didn't seem fitting for someone with sixty-seven years of life experience. Don't get me wrong, though – I don't mean that in a nasty way. In fact, I found it quite endearing. It's just that she would have never acted in such a way when she was an old woman. She certainly wouldn't have considered armed robbery. I guessed she must have been adapting to her new youth more adeptly than I'd realised. Or was she? After all, on the first night when Mutsuko was an old woman, it was she who proposed we talk sex across the partition. You could say that it was a lot more radical for an old woman to propose that than a young one. So maybe she really hadn't changed so much at all.

'Wouldn't it be better to rest all that on a newspaper?'

'I don't have any newspapers.'

'A magazine would work.'

'I don't have any magazines, either.'

'What do you do when you eat here?'

'I don't.'

'How about when you drink whisky?'

'I leave the bottle by the sink, make a whisky with water there and bring it over here.'

'Let's do that, then.'

We went over to the sink together and she let me use the only glass there was, as if it were perfectly normal. Perhaps that is the value of a sixty-seven-year-old woman. But then again, maybe that's exactly what a young girl would do too. It's not as if I knew much about young women.

'Listen. I'm not trying to talk you out of it. But, of course, I guess I would say that. Anyway, I want you to know that I'm not saying this for moral reasons or out of fear. Well, maybe there's some fear. It's just that I think armed robbery is . . . kind of piti-ful. I mean, it's not as if we need the money. It's just that you want to use the pistol.'

'Are you going to suggest that I go up into the mountains and shoot it there instead?'

'I'm not saying that. Look, don't take me as a fool. I've dropped too far out of society to think that. And I've experienced plenty of the pain that comes with the fall, so there's not that much stopping me from rebelling against society. I'm going to drink this.'

'Go ahead.'

Without ice, it felt like a cheap drink. It didn't even taste good.

'How about we walk into a cinema without paying,' I said, proposing an idea that had been playing on my mind.

'A cinema?' she said, as if in disbelief.

'Yes.'

'Sneaking into a cinema instead of staging an armed rob-bery?'

'I asked you not to take me for a fool. Let me finish.'

'Okay.'

'We flash the pistol and walk in through the front entrance. If anybody tries to stop us, we can shoot the window or some-thing and prove that the gun is loaded with real bullets.'

'And we watch the film?'

'Of course not. If we did that, a bus would arrive to take us away.'

'Not a truck?'

'It might be a truck.'

'A truck would be better. Policemen piling out of a truck.'

'But the police won't have the chance to arrive in a truck or bus. We'll simply rip one poster off the wall and escape out of the back exit.

'So it's just a game.'

'A game if we get away with it. But a crime if we get caught. It's easier said than done. We're going to take a pistol out in public. That alone will be nerve-racking. To shoot it will be even more daring. Think about it . . . what would you do if the audience at the cinema noticed the shot? If they came running out into the foyer? We'd have to make sure not to shoot anyone. So we'd have to fire a shot into the ceiling. It would cause a panic. People would faint. To find the back exit in a situation like that may well be tougher than succeeding in an armed robbery.'

'Are there any back exits in cinemas?'

'There must be.'

'Isn't the end of the foyer usually just the toilets?'

Now that she mentioned it, I got the feeling it was.

'And even if there was a back exit, it would probably be locked.'

My plan was falling apart just like that.

'I was thinking that there would be an office at the end of the foyer, and that there would be a door that opened up to the side street.'

'Okay, let's do it,' she said.

'But there probably isn't a cinema like that.'

'That's okay. We'll have a pistol on us. We can leave from anywhere we want.'

'What if the only way to leave without a key is to go through the front entrance? We'd be forced to go back through the panicking crowd.'

'We'd have a pistol on us. Nobody would challenge us. We'll just have to do it quickly and disappear before the police arrive.'

'That's true, but–'

'What time is it?'

'Eight forty-five.'

'Let's go.'

'Now?'

'Well most of the performances will end soon after nine.'

'You want to do this tonight?'

'Would you prefer to do it during the day tomorrow?'

'No, but I mean the cinema will still be there tomorrow night.'

'But I might not be.'

'That–'

'–might not happen. But then again it might.'

Mutsuko picked up the Colt, then walked over and turned the light off, leaving the light from the window and from the room with the sink as the only illumination.

'Shouldn't we think about this a little more?'

'About what?'

'About . . . how we should hide our faces, for example.'

'There's no time for that.'

She reached out her right hand towards me.

'What?'

'You hold it,' she said, pushing me the Colt.

'Oh . . . right.'

I felt like I was about to grasp a live electric cable, but I didn't feel I could say no.

'We should hurry.'

Mutsuko opened the door, then turned off the light in the

room with the sink. Becoming nothing more than a silhouette saying 'hurry', she dashed off down the stairs. I had no choice but to run after her. I had to think quickly of somewhere to put the gun. I thought of putting it in my pocket, but I was afraid it might go off if I jolted it, so instead I kept it in my hand and held it flat against my chest under my suit jacket.

Outside, Mutsuko was waiting, immediately trotting off down the narrow hill as soon as I caught up. But why was she making me carry the pistol? This whole thing had started only because *she'd* said she wanted to use it. Because *she'd* wanted to shoot it. So why was it me carrying it? Should I tell her to hold it herself, since it was she who wanted to do this? And even if I did, we were already among the crowds of Miyamasuzaka, so I couldn't just pass it to her on the street.

Just as when I'd chased her earlier in the evening, Mutsuko moved quickly and determinedly through the crowds. She didn't seem at all concerned about me behind her, either. In fact, if I'd stopped in my tracks, she'd probably have kept walking and not realised until she reached the cinema. Maybe I should stop, I thought. Surely it was crazy to do something like this without a real plan? And no matter that it was concealed beneath my jacket, the fact remained that I was carrying a pistol. What would happen if I flipped open my suit jacket? If people saw me: a man with a gun running after a woman – that's how it would have appeared. This in itself was a huge deal, an experience unmatched in my entire life, but on top of that I was about to go and point that gun at someone.

I wanted to think this all through a little more. If we thought about it, we might not be willing to do it any more. I mean, it wasn't something that we actually *had* to do. And, of course, if we were talking only about me, then this was something I didn't want to do at all. So it was utterly meaningless for me to be holding the pistol. I really needed to give it to her. But where? How?

We stopped at a red light and Mutsuko suddenly turned round.

'What time is it?'

I caught my breath as sweat streamed out of me.

'Is something the matter?' she asked, and I saw a couple of strangers glance at me.

'Eight fifty-seven,' I said, looking at the watch on my left wrist, then I gave her a smile. When she'd turned round, she'd surprised me, making my hand unconsciously grip the gun tighter. Luckily the safety was on as my finger was on the trigger. If it hadn't been, I'd have just shot through the shoulder of my jacket.

Mutsuko and the people around us started walking. Falling one step behind, I quickly followed. I was feeling a little overcome by her assertiveness and by my willingness to go along with it. Up until now, I'd been tolerant of her ego and had made an exception of her in terms of my usual cynicism and general dislike of women. But now as I stared at her back, I sensed the same selfishness I saw in my wife; I didn't want our relationship to become like that.

Mutsuko suddenly came to a stop. We were already in front of the cinema. It was the largest or second largest in Shibuya. I had been there a long time ago, but I couldn't remember what the structure was like inside.

'So, shall we?' said Mutsuko.

'Yes, but . . .' I said, shaking my suit jacket. 'I need to hand this over,' I said, keeping my voice down.

'Hand what over?'

'The pistol.'

'To who?'

'You.'

'No, you hold it.'

'But then you can't use it.'

'I don't need to use it. I'll leave it to you.'

'Leave it to me?'

'It was your idea. You can use it. You go ahead of me.'

'Huh?'

'You go first.'

'But—'

'It would be strange if a woman went first.'

'I don't think so.'

'Look, we're wasting time, debating like this. The film could end soon. And this'll be much more difficult once loads of people are coming out.'

I had no choice but to head for the entrance.

Women were like that – crying out for equality one second, then hiding behind the man and nudging him in the back the next. And she'd said it was my idea! Well, maybe it was, but I only suggested it to stop her from committing armed robbery, not because I *wanted* to do it. And the ticket counter seemed to be closed anyway, so there was nobody to collect tickets.

'There isn't anybody here,' I said.

'There,' said Mutsuko from behind me.

There was a man in the corner of the lobby standing on a stepladder and reaching for the ceiling. A woman who appeared to be assisting him was standing below him.

'Looks like they're changing a light bulb,' said Mutsuko.

'What should we do?'

'What?'

'What should I say?'

'What do you mean, what should you say?'

'Well, I can't just go over there, flash this at them and say we're heading to the back, can I?'

'What do you want to do, then? It's no good asking me.'

If this was what she was like, I don't know if it really was the husband's fault that they got divorced.

'Yes?' came a voice from the distance. It was the woman by the stepladder.

'Is there something I can help you with?' she asked, her voice raised slightly.

'Um, no. Will the film be ending soon?'

'In about five minutes.'

'Oh, right, it's okay then.'

I stepped outside.

'What are you doing?' Mutsuko chased after me.

'We have to think of something else.'

'We could go to the office. Rob the day's earnings and run.'

'We can't do that.'

'Then what do you suggest?'

'I'm thinking.'

'Well, people are going to be streaming out in about five minutes, so you had better think fast.'

'Me? Why is it down to me?'

'You didn't like my idea. So it's only natural that I ask your thoughts.'

'Hey, I was the one who didn't want to do anything!'

'Why are you bringing that up now? I only did what you wanted to do!'

I started walking towards the entrance again.

'What are we going to do?'

I didn't know what to do, but I felt it would be better to do something than to keep arguing or to do nothing. I walked into the lobby and headed straight for the man and woman who were putting away the stepladder. They noticed me coming towards them and looked in my direction. I immediately pointed the pistol at them. Both of them looked completely confused.

'This isn't a model. It's real,' I said. 'If you don't believe me, I can shoot something.'

I glanced around quickly to find something I could shoot.

'We believe you. You don't have to shoot anything,' spluttered the man.

He was tall, thin and young, and I was surprised by the tension in his voice. I hadn't imagined that people would believe that it was real so easily. I thought we might have to go through some frustrating, pointless exchange.

'You believe me?' I asked, in spite of myself.

'I do.'

'Yes,' nodded the woman, who was standing there looking like she didn't know what to do.

'Fine then. Go to the end.'

'Huh?'

'To the end. You go first.'

'By end you mean . . .?'

'Over there.'

'There's only the bathroom down there.'

'I know that. Both of you go first.'

'What's the matter, Kobayashi?' came the thick voice of a man from behind me.

I pointed the pistol in the direction of the voice and a fat middle-aged man in a suit stopped in his tracks about ten metres away.

'Don't move. Or I'll shoot.'

Suddenly I was pushed hard from behind. I staggered.

'Call 110!' screamed the man behind me.

I stumbled forward two or three steps, then caught my balance and turned round. The man and woman were running towards the end of the foyer. I pointed the gun in their direction and pulled the trigger. Fortunately, the safety was on. I had been half aware that it was, and that it was better that way, and I then turned towards the middle-aged man – catching a glimpse of his back as he ran into the office near the entrance.

'Let's get out of here!' Mutsuko screamed. Of course, it was obvious that was what we needed to do, but instead I headed in the direction of the man and woman.

'Over here,' shouted Mutsuko. But I ignored her and kept running in the same direction. The man and woman weren't out in the hallway. They'd probably run into the bathroom, and as I ran I kept my eyes on the walls, reaching out for a poster when I got to the end of the foyer.

'We don't need it!' I heard Mutsuko cry out behind me.

My hand slipped and I couldn't grab it. It was kept inside a glass case. It would take time to lift the glass casing off and remove the poster, so I turned back, bumped into Mutsuko and said, 'Excuse me,' immediately noticing how panicked I must have been to say such a thing at a time like this. By now, there was nobody in the lobby and the door to the office that the middle-aged man had run into was closed.

We ran through the front entrance and out into the street, then headed for Miyamasuzaka. I almost bumped into several people. Then, suddenly realising that I hadn't hidden the pistol, I quickly shoved it under the front of my jacket.

We got to the top of the hill and looked for an alleyway. To get back to Mutsuko's place, we realised we'd have to cross the road, but there was no way we could risk waiting at a red light. I looked around for an alleyway in which to hide, but I couldn't see one anywhere. So I wondered if it might be best if we just kept running. At least that way we could get further away.

'Wait,' came Mutsuko's voice. 'I can't run any more.'

'But it's turning green!' I called back, trying to encourage her, then I made for the pedestrian crossing at the top of the hill. Mutsuko staggered after me, holding the side of her stomach. But we couldn't afford to take a break. Not yet. I ran over the crossing, then turned round and waited for her. Once she'd crossed over, we headed down a hill and looked for a dark path. I made a left turn, then jogged down a back street with Mutsuko calling out 'Wait!' behind me.

It was okay if she trailed behind until I found a place for us to catch our breath. But I couldn't find anywhere that would do. Instead I found an empty lot with a big tarpaulin covering the side facing the road.

'Here!' I turned and gestured to Mutsuko, who was still trailing behind, then I peeked in through the corner. It appeared to be the site of a house that had recently been demolished. There was still a small bulldozer taking up about a quarter of the area. I checked the street and saw no one.

'Let's go in,' I whispered to Mutsuko, who was now in earshot. But she ignored me and went right by, still holding the side of her stomach.

'Don't you want to rest?' I said, chasing after her.

'We can be at my place in less than a minute,' she replied sharply.

We weren't as close as she said, but moving as fast as we could, we reached her place about three minutes later.

'You kept running on and on by yourself. Not even pulling me along by the hand!' said Mutsuko, sitting down on the sofa and kicking the cardboard box in front of her. I guess even sixty-seven-year-olds do things like that if they have the strength to do so.

I sat down on the bed. Finally letting go of the pistol, I opened and closed my hand repeatedly to relieve the stiffness.

'I can't believe you could even think of taking a poster instead of running away,' said Mutsuko, glaring at me.

'That was the plan.'

'But there was no point. You surprised me, running to the back instead of running away!'

'I wanted to go as far as I could.'

'Then you should have taken the poster. Instead you just touched the glass, then ran away ahead of me.'

'I thought that was as far as I could go.'

'You should have taken a shot or two. Then they would have been more obedient.'

'If that's what you wanted, then you should have taken the gun. I did try to give it to you!'

'I felt bad, making a man follow me unprotected.'

'Oh come on!'

'Really, I did. What if I'd just run off and made you follow? You'd have been hurt, wouldn't you?'

'No I wouldn't. It's easy to do nothing at the time and then criticise afterwards.'

'Well, what could I have done? What could I have done there?'

'You hardly said a thing.'

'What did you want me to say? Don't criticise me just because you couldn't do it right.'

'It's not that I didn't do it right. I did more than enough. And on top of that, we were able to get back here without getting caught. I would say it was pretty successful.'

'But they saw our faces.'

'Well, there was no way for us to hide them. You're the one who rushed us into it. You rushed me, saying a crowd of people would be coming out in five minutes.'

'Now I'm worried. I'm worried about you. You could get caught tomorrow if you go out.'

'There's no point in worrying. I don't mean to sound funny, but I have a very typical face. As long as I'm not caught in the act, I think I can get away by just pretending I know nothing about it.'

'Don't use that tone with me. I'm just worried about you.' Her voice weakened and broke. Then she started to cry. Unable to take it any longer, I stood up and walked over to the kitchen and poured myself a whisky with water.

I didn't want to get into an argument like this, with her of all people. An argument just like those I have with my wife or the other woman I once had an affair with. I didn't want an argument like this, not with Mutsuko. But even though her circumstances were exceptional, to say the least, it didn't change the fact she was a woman. It was pure sentiment to wish for a different kind of relationship, and to feel disappointed when it didn't go the way I hoped.

'Do you want a drink?' I asked. 'A whisky?'

There was no response. Given that I was making the effort to patch things up, you'd have thought the least she could do was respond.

'Do you want a whisky?' I asked again.

'Yes, I'll have one.'

She said this in a voice that was barely audible, but I could tell that she didn't want to argue any more either. I poured whisky and water into the teacup and returned to the room. Mutsuko had moved from the sofa to the bed, where I had been sitting until just moments ago. She was holding the pistol. I handed the whisky to Mutsuko and she took it in her left hand, while thanking me in a small voice. I sat down on the sofa, leaned my head against the back of it and closed my eyes in an attempt to relax. But the adrenalin was still flowing and I couldn't even feel the fatigue. I thought I'd gradually feel tired if I drank the whisky.

When I opened my eyes the pistol was pointed right at me, with Mutsuko's pale face behind it. I immediately sensed it wasn't a joke, but I managed to make a wry smile anyway and say, 'Stop it now. It's not a nice feeling.'

'Don't move,' she said, her voice quivering.

I stayed completely still. I wanted to say something, but I couldn't find the words. Mutsuko stood up slowly and threw away the cup in her left hand while keeping the gun, her right hand and her face trained on me – as if her left side were somehow acting independently, unaware of the actions of the rest of her body.

'What are you thinking?' I said, finally opening my mouth.

'If you move, I'll shoot. I honestly will,' she said, keeping her eyes on my forehead. The barrel of the gun slowly came closer.

'I don't care if I die,' I said. And I meant it. I didn't feel like fighting for my life. I had suddenly given up on everything. There probably wouldn't be much to look forward to even if I did keep living, and Mutsuko had already given me plenty to be glad about.

'I've started to feel that feeling,' said Mutsuko.

'But–'

'Don't look. Don't look at me,' she screamed.

I felt something strike me in the head. She had hit me with the pistol. Then I felt it again. And again. And again. I shouted out and felt like my voice belonged to someone else. I felt blood running down my forehead and into my eyes. Then nothing. Nothing but darkness.

5

Of the rolls of film on which I'd photographed Mutsuko, I took the two twenty-four-exposure ones photographed outside to a photo shop inside Shinjuku station on the Odakyu Line and got forty-nine pictures developed. Mutsuko could be clearly seen in each of them. Well, most of them, anyway – I must admit a few were rather out of focus.

I'd been wearing a bandage on my head for a couple of weeks and I still occasionally had the feeling that Mutsuko might be nothing more than a product of my imagination. Whenever I did feel that way, I'd open my commuter-pass holder and take a look at a shot of Mutsuko that had turned out particularly well – one I'd taken on the corner of the Mitsui building. There were also many times when I'd suddenly get the urge to look at the image while I was on a train. When I felt that way, I'd get pleasure out of resisting the temptation to look until I had reached my station.

When I'd regained consciousness that day, Mutsuko had already gone, so I caught a taxi home. The bleeding from my head hadn't been too bad and a towel had been wrapped around the wound. Both at the company and at home, I'd gotten away with the lie that I'd been attacked while I was drunk.

Although I couldn't go so far as to say I'd appreciated her kindness in wrapping a towel around my head, I couldn't find it

in myself to be angry with Mutsuko. After all, I could understand her not wanting others to see her transformation in
progress. Instead, I simply wondered where she'd gone and felt
sorry for her, knowing she'd have to find somewhere to stay on
her own.

In the middle of June the company suddenly undertook a
restructuring, and the built-to-order projects department was
abolished just like that. My new post was acting head of the
public relations research section. Despite the name, however,
we didn't actually have our own section, but instead occupied a
couple of desks in the corner of Headquarters' public relations
department. Me and my one subordinate were supposed to
'liaise' (run errands, in other words) between the sales staff at
the housing exhibits and the members of the public relations
department. Our days consisted of going from one housing
exhibit to another, covering all eleven exhibits in Saitama,
Chiba, Tokyo and Kanagawa between just the two of us. It was-
n't meaningless work and I didn't slack off. But I didn't regain
any desire for promotion or feel any sense of renewed loyalty to
the company. All I was concerned about was how I could see
Mutsuko again and how I could develop the nude photographs
of her I'd taken that night in the hotel room. I had, after all,
purposely taken those shots in black and white as I'd thought it
would make them easier to develop. But now that I actually
wanted to do so, I was finding it considerably more difficult to
get them done than I'd imagined.

I went to a camera enthusiast's store to see an exhibition of
do-it-yourself darkrooms. I'd even asked the sales assistant
about the possibility of developing photographs without a
darkroom, but it sounded like it'd be difficult to carry the

materials into my home unnoticed. It would have looked suspicious if I rather suddenly took a new interest in photography and, considering that development involved steps such as 'running the film under the tap for thirty minutes' or 'hanging the negatives up to dry naturally in the room', it would take an extraordinary amount of excuses to develop the pictures and it'd be highly likely that my wife would find them. If that happened, I'd not only have the shame of being found with pictures of a naked woman and her private parts, but she'd also find out about the affair. In the end, unable to do anything with them, I put the two twenty-four-exposure films of Mutsuko naked in a paper bag with the negatives and prints of Mutsuko taken outside, then stashed them away in my desk at work.

As for my wife, she'd reached a point where she could no longer manage her town magazine with just three members of staff, and she began looking for additional help by recruiting 'members' – calling on people to do editing, research, distribution and ad sales for no pay.

'It'll mean I won't be able to secure an income for myself like before, but the money that comes in will still belong to the company,' she explained, sounding a little defensive. But of course I was fully in favour of it. If she had that kind of organisational ability, I could respect her for it. And the more she left me alone, the less guilty I'd feel about the things I was doing. It seemed to me that the best thing the two of us could do was to maintain this slightly distant relationship until our old age.

'But are there really people who are willing to work for no pay?'

'There are. Some places even charge a membership fee and they still get lots of members. It's a question of whether we can provide them with tasks that they find truly challenging and rewarding.'

I was a little stunned to hear my wife say this kind of thing seriously. I had thought that it was a way of gathering bored old women and coaxing them into providing free labour, but that kind of thought wasn't in my wife's mind at all. I felt inferior somehow and was careful not to make any sarcastic comments. I had no right to be critical of her anyway. This new passion of hers was a lot healthier than the things occupying my mind.

I mean, what was I doing? I was taking out Mutsuko's photo from my commuter-pass wallet under the tables of cafés and staring at it. And I was chasing young girls with my eyes. Well, chasing for one girl in particular, as I'd become convinced that the Mutsuko I would next see would be a girl – only I didn't know how old she would be now. There didn't seem to be any strict pattern in the way she went from being sixty-seven to forty and then to her mid twenties. Would she appear as a teenage girl or maybe even younger? It was abnormal to be thinking such things, but thinking back on what I had experienced, it seemed to me like a perfectly natural prediction. On the other hand, there were also times when a sharp sense of fear skimmed my chest. A fear that I might never see her again. I tried not to think such thoughts, as it brought on an unbearable feeling of solitude. But I couldn't help thinking about how much she'd enriched my life. And when I thought of this, I could easily forgive her for the hard-headedness she'd shown on our last evening together. I could be very understanding when it came to Mutsuko. If only she'd appear. If only she'd show me her face. To stop this hopeless feeling of need that was consuming me through my waking and sleeping hours.

It was a rainy night in early July. The official end of the rainy season had been followed by three hot, sunny days, but the rain had returned that Saturday. The temperature was too cool to just be in short sleeves and I was wearing a summer jacket in the living room of a show home – our company's Scandinavian-style two-storey house in a large housing exhibit located along Loop No. 8 in Yoga, to be exact. The sparse flow of visitors completely stopped after 8 p.m. and though it was decided that we would stay open until 9 p.m. on the summer weekends, there was nothing you could do when it rained like this. So I let the two young sales guys leave at eight, but as for me, I had no reason to rush home.

'There was a time when I used to be in sales. I can manage for an hour on my own.' That's what I told the two, as they'd already worked hard enough for the day. They wouldn't have been allowed to claim overtime even if they had stayed, as the logic at our company for people in sales was unchanging – dictating that 'You can't do your job properly if you start claiming overtime pay.' Bearing this in mind, you had to call it a day whenever you could.

I looked up at my reflection in the large sash window facing the garden. It was light inside, so you could hardly see the garden except for a small area through the bottom left corner of the four-pane window that was illuminated by a small garden light by the front door. There I was, staring at myself sitting on the sofa. A thin, middle-aged man on a brand-new but cheap living-room sofa gazing at his reflection. My hair was short. Just long enough to be parted. It had been clipped down to just a couple of centimetres so that my head wound could be treated and the rest of my hair had been trimmed to match the length.

I was told that I should just keep it like that for the summer. But instead of going to a barber again, I had let it grow out and parted it once more.

Suddenly my heart jumped and I realised why I had been drawn to look out of the window. I had felt a presence in the garden. But as I couldn't see the garden very well, I'd been staring at myself instead. There was something on the other side of me, or more precisely, inside of me. I looked harder and saw someone standing on the other side of my reflection. Though I couldn't see very well, I was already filled with anticipation and almost fell over as I stood up. I managed to steady myself by leaning my right hand on the sofa, but then I hit my shin against the glass table in front of the sofa as I ran over to the light switch.

Thinking back, it was a strange thing to do. If I'd wanted to check if someone was there, I should have gone to the window and slid it open. But instead I had run towards the light switch. Perhaps I was afraid of opening the windows and suddenly coming face to face with Mutsuko. Whatever my reason, I flicked off all three switches and was confronted by a girl in the garden.

From the dark of the living room I could see what appeared to be a ghostly girl holding an umbrella silhouetted by the white of the garden light. I couldn't make out her face, but I could tell she was looking at me. I moved away from the light switch and slowly, carefully, walked over to the window. I guessed this skinny girl must have been in high school.

I went to open the window.

'Good evening,' said Mutsuko. Her voice that of a young girl.

'Good evening,' I responded. She was beautiful. Tears welled up in my eyes and, unable even to ask her to come in, and with my eyes still on her, I began to sob. Mutsuko watched me in silence.

'I cried too,' said Mutsuko, in her young girl's voice.

'Did you?'

I handed her a cloth at the front door to the show house and she wiped her feet, her white arms showing from her short-sleeved blouse and her calves looking painfully thin.

'Aren't you cold?'

'I am.'

I took off my jacket and put it round her. Mutsuko pulled it over herself without any protest and let me guide her into the living room.

'I'll make some coffee. Or would you like tea better?'

I was unconsciously speaking to her like I would to a young girl.

'I'll take tea, thank you,' she said as she sat down on a chair, striking me with her adult speech.

I moved towards the sideboard in the corner of the living room, where there was some instant coffee as well as green and black tea.

'How did you know to find me here?'

'I made a phone call. And I was told you would probably be here.'

'I was worried you might not find me. Both my phone number and office have changed.'

Mutsuko nodded and pulled my jacket closer around her chest.

'Do you have a fever?'

She shook her head without looking at me.

'Just tired.'

'If only we had something to eat, like biscuits.'

Even as I poured the tea, I kept looking at this girl in front of me, feeling a need to keep an eye on her. This Mutsuko who sat motionless with her eyes on the floor exuded a beauty completely different from before: a pure kind of beauty, with everything unnecessary removed. Absent was the unsure feeling of a teenager. Missing was the clumsiness of a child. Instead this young beauty possessed the grace and refinement of sixty-seven years of life experience. I'm sure my perceptions were coloured in her favour, but the way in which she wiped her feet at the front entrance charmed me in a way that a normal cute girl could not. Maybe it was her casual yet efficient hand movements that drew me in and the way they seemed so adult.

'I did a terrible thing,' said the girl.

'What did you do?'

I thought she'd done something and needed my help.

'No, I did something terrible to you.' She smiled and shot me a glance.

Inside, I knew it was her, but still I felt unsure of how to respond to the young girl in front of me who was apologising for something done by the Mutsuko in her twenties.

'It's okay,' I said.

'But are *you* okay?'

'I'm okay. Now, anyway.'

'I didn't know what else to do. You wouldn't have been able to leave if I had lost consciousness there, and I didn't want that. I'm not sure exactly how, but I'm quite certain that there must be a stage of my transformation that is pretty ugly. That's something I don't want to share with anyone. Perhaps like the way an elephant goes into hiding when it knows that it's dying, I myself feel an instinct to retreat from the world. It's a feeling so strong, I'll do anything to hide myself. But afterwards, I couldn't bear the thought of the terrible thing I did to you. How I could have killed you. I wanted to apologise.'

I found it refreshing how this girl of sixteen or seventeen years could address me as if we were equals, with the words and gestures of an adult.

'I took two days off work, and the big bandage came off after a week. It wasn't a matter of life and death.'

I handed her the tea. She held the cup with the fingertips of both hands and warmed her face with the steam from the cup, as if it were the middle of winter.

'You need to get something like a summer cardigan,' I said.

'Yes. I'm not used to this season yet.'

'Well, you probably won't need a raincoat, anyway.'

'This is funny.'

'What is?'

'It's like we're in your home.'

'My house isn't this tidy. It's not this big, either. There's stuff all over the place. Once you actually live in a place, there's no way you can keep it this neat.'

'Are you sure you won't get into trouble, saying that kind of thing?'

She sounded like a young girl when she said that.

'I have to stay here for about another ten minutes. Then I have to put down the shutters, turn off the lights upstairs and down here, then lock up and we can go for something nice to eat.'

'Are you hungry?'

'Well, you look like you are.'

'Why don't we just stay here?'

'The security guard will be coming round. My company might find out.'

'I suppose they'd fire you if they found out you stayed the night with a high-schooler.'

She looked every bit like she was in high school. There had been one time when I'd seen a person I knew for the first time in a long time, and I'd felt like crying when I saw how much that person had aged. But at this moment in time, I knew I wasn't witnessing the powerlessness of people against ageing. I was watching the futility of a person against the onslaught of youth.

'Since when?' I asked. 'I mean, how long have you been the way you are now?'

'This is the tenth day.'

I nodded. I had thought that I had managed to say it without any expression, but I could sense from Mutsuko's voice that she was trying to comfort me.

'It wasn't that I was seeing anyone else or anything of that sort. It's just that it's not easy getting used to myself. When you're this age there are a lot of obstacles to face when trying to live by yourself. You can't even rent an apartment on your own.'

'So what did you do about an apartment?'

'I rented it when I was in my twenties, so I'm okay for now. It's so funny to hear myself say that. When I was in my twenties.'

'Is there anything I can do for you?'

'There is.'

'What is it?'

'I want to stay at a hotel and splurge on room service.'

'Sure.'

I didn't have that kind of money on me, but I would do whatever I had to.

'I have money. But you can't really do that kind of thing alone at this age.'

'I know.'

'So shall we go?'

'Huh?'

'Can we go to the hotel now?'

'Right. Okay. Just as soon as I lock the place up.'

'Can you stay the night?'

'Yes.'

'Then you should call home. Tell them you won't be coming back tonight.'

'I'll do it later.'

'Do it now.'

'It's not easy for me to say this, but I don't want you to hear me talking to my wife.'

'All right. I think that's a good thing.'

'What do you mean?'

'That you have a life that doesn't have anything to do with me. One that you don't want to jeopardise. I'm not criticising you. I have a life like that too, and I don't want you to intrude on it. I don't even want to talk about it.'

'I'll go and close the shutters upstairs.'

'I want to see what it's like up there.'

We went up the stairs together and Mutsuko cried a little when she saw the child's room. At first I thought it was because she was thinking of her own children. But that wasn't the case. It was because the room was designed for a teenage girl. It had a pretty random layout and there was a Western doll sitting on a bed with pink covers, a mobile hanging from the ceiling and a reproduction of a Marie Laurencin painting on the wall. But for some reason it suddenly had Mutsuko in tears.

'What's the matter?' I said, moving to open the windows so I could close the shutters.

'Just my emotions,' she said. I could tell she was trying to be blasé about it, but her voice was still tearful.

'I guess they're affected quite strongly by the physical. I sometimes react like a young girl. I was thinking how nice it would be if I could continue to live my life as I am, here in this room.'

I nodded, closed the shutters and windows, then went over to where she stood, near the bed with her head hanging low, and put a fatherly arm round her shoulders. And when I rubbed her back through my suit jacket that was so big on her, I could tell that she was also very thin.

I had given up all hope of forging a connection with my own child. But I really wished I could take this girl somewhere and raise her. I felt the warmth of her body. Then, contrary to those feelings, a heat began to well up around my crotch and I quickly moved away.

'Which hotel do you want to stay at?'

Mutsuko named the hotel we had stayed in before.

With the name of that place came memories of our affair and the excitement of it all. But I was reluctant to speak of it to such a young girl. So I simply said, 'Let's go there, then.' Of course, I knew she wasn't a young girl inside and I knew my reluctance made no sense. But looking at this pure, untainted girl before my eyes, they were feelings I couldn't suppress.

The rain began to fall harder by the time we caught a cab and occasionally there was lightning and thunder in the distance. Our room was on the thirty-second floor and it had a view of this endless city. I watched as the lightning cut a streak in the distance and I listened to the thunder that followed. As soon as we'd walked into the room, Mutsuko had glued herself to the window, saying, 'I want to see an even bigger lightning strike.' Watching her from behind, she looked like a teenager who had run away from home with nothing more than the clothes on her back. It was a thought that turned me on.

'I think maybe we have a problem,' I said, looking for the room-service menu.

'What?'

'It's the way you're getting excited about lightning. It makes me feel like you're . . . a real girl.'

'I am a real girl,' she replied, turning round and looking at me with mischievous eyes. 'Is there a part of me that you would say isn't?'

'A real girl wouldn't talk like that.'

'Really? How would she talk?'

'Look, here's the menu. Get whatever you want. It'll be my treat.'

'It's okay.'

'Even if it is okay, please let me at least get this.'

'You saying that makes it hard to say–'

'It's all right. I can afford room service for one night.'

'It's not that. Like I said earlier, I'm not that hungry.'

'You can pay if you want.'

'Really, that has nothing to do with it. I'm being honest. I want to splurge, but I think my stomach has shrunk. I don't think I'll be able to eat much. I just want a little alcohol and a prawn cocktail.'

'How about a Shalyapin steak?'

'No thank you.'

'Well, you can't call it splurging if we only get one thing.'

'Then how about the caviar and smoked salmon?'

'This menu doesn't have anything special on it.'

'Yes, but just that would come to over 20,000 yen.'

I didn't know much about wine, so I ordered a bottle of the most expensive white on the menu with two plates each of three dishes.

'Have you ever read *Demian*?' asked Mutsuko.

'By Hermann Hesse?'

'Yes.'

'I have, but way back in my schooldays, I think. I hardly remember any of it now.'

'Why don't we try to remember it?'

'Let's do that. When I'm with you, I can do things that I couldn't before.'

'I wonder about that.'

'After all, I was able to speak French.'

'Yes, but your attempt at being a poster thief was quite miserable.'

'That's because I'd never done that kind of thing before. It can't be helped if I'm awkward at something I do for the first time. I was thinking afterwards about how I used to practise kendo in school. I wasn't good enough to enter the Tokyo tournament or anything. But at my prime, I was able to beat the guys in my team two out of three times. If I had taken a wooden sword with me instead of a pistol, the ability I had cultivated in the past might have come back to life. Who knows, I might have been even more impressive than then.'

'So how is it coming along?'

'How is what coming along?'

'*Demian.*'

I put my wine glass down and composed myself, but I could only remember the words on the cover of the book and not a single line from the story itself. Perhaps I hadn't read it after all.

'I feel like I'd be able to remember *Beneath the Wheel* or *Peter Camenzind.*'

'Different, aren't I, now that I'm an "adolescent"?' Mutsuko giggled. 'Bringing up *Demian.*'

'That's true.'

'Each human being represents a unique and valuable experiment on the part of nature.'

'Is that from *Demian*?'

'Yes.' She continued, 'Only once and never again. That is why every person's story is worthy of every consideration.'

'Of course, *your* story certainly deserves every consideration.'

'That's not what I'm alluding to. Of course, if I had more time, it wouldn't be so bad to tell a lot of people about what happened to me and then die amidst all the commotion. But I don't have that kind of time.'

When I looked into this girl's thoughtful eyes, I knew that anything I could say would seem to be little more than lip service. As a result, I said nothing. I just gave a small nod instead.

'God, or whatever it is that's making me go through this experience, may be devoid of reason, goodwill, ill will, or any will at all. Whatever is doing this may be capricious, merciless, or kind. It may even just be toying with me, but I have both reason and will, so all I can do is use that to counter it in what small way I can.'

'Is there anything I can do at all? If there is, just say the word and I'll do it.'

Mutsuko smiled. 'It's okay. Don't look at me like I'm on my deathbed. To be honest, I don't feel like I'm going to die soon. Normally, when somebody dies of illness, their body deteriorates and they probably eventually come to accept it. But I'm becoming younger and younger. Healthier and stronger. My skin is unbelievably young and in my mind I know that if I keep going like this I'll turn into a baby next, and it frightens me to think of the future. But at the same time, there's a part of me that can't take it seriously. I mean, look at me. I'm healthy from head to toe.'

Mutsuko stopped talking and put a prawn in her mouth with a thin fork. I couldn't say anything. All I knew was that it helped when she was able to remain positive in some way.

'I want words,' said Mutsuko, out of the blue.

'Words?'

'Some kind of words. Encouraging words. Words that will help me come to terms with this incomprehensible destiny, words that will cheer me up, words that will make me laugh, words that will move me. Say anything. Say anything that comes to your mind.'

That's when I realised that I didn't possess any appropriate words. I thought that in order to comfort someone in Mutsuko's situation, I needed words that touched the very core of something. But no such words came to mind. All I could recall were memories of trying to respond to people with funny, witty, or clever words. And when I thought about it, I realised I hadn't even been doing that recently. I wondered what words Christ, Mohammed, or the Buddha would prepare for a girl like Mutsuko. They probably had just the right words, but as I'd never seriously studied any of their teachings, there was no way they would come to mind. There was probably a bible in the desk drawer of our hotel room, but I couldn't look for it and read it here and now. Wasn't there something, anything I could say? Words that could comfort Mutsuko and give her strength? I tried desperately to fumble through my memories, to mine them for the right words.

'Is something the matter?' she asked me.

'Words. I'm trying to remember words.'

'Are you crying?'

'No, of course not.'

'Then what kind of words?'

'I'm still trying to think of something to say.'

'That's a lie. You had something in your mind. I want to hear it.'

Then at that moment, words came to mind.

'There was this book by a young French critic called Bosch that came out when I was a student.'

'Yes?'

'He said, "I want to criticise the young authors that bear a grudge towards love and write pretentiously about how empty it is".'

'Criticise them how?'

'He asked what they wanted to substitute it with.'

'I see.'

'That's all. I don't know what else I can say. All I can do is care for you.'

'Thank you.'

'You could say that this is nothing but sweet talk,' I continued. 'That I may not be able to really care for you the way you can yourself. Much of what I'm feeling now is probably sentimental and false. But I don't want to keep picking at my feelings and thinking about myself all the time. Albert Camus said, "We don't have the time to completely be ourselves. We only have the room to be happy." I don't know how he was feeling when he said that, but these words are perfect for us now. I don't want to analyse myself and make an issue of whether my feelings are real or not. I just want to care for you. I want to concentrate on you like crazy.'

'That makes me happy.'

'Charles de Gaulle said to André Malraux . . . Never mind, it's stupid.'

'No, what did he say?'

'It's not the kind of thing to talk about while drinking good wine.'

'There's no reason why we should let the wine decide our conversation. I want to hear anything you have to say. What did de Gaulle say?' said this young girl. It was so cute that it made my heart tremble.

'He said, "In the end, only death wins."'

'That sounds a little too obvious a point to make.'

'Yes, but Malraux responded.'

'And what did he say?'

'"Is it not more important that death does not win instantly?"'

I noticed that the rain had stopped. The lightning flashed faintly in the clouds that hung over the distant mountains.

'He's right. I have to think like that and make the most of what little time I have.'

I felt that I was shallow for not being able to respond to such a clear and deep thought. I remembered that Goethe had said to Charlotte von Stein, 'My merits are increasing, but my virtues are decreasing.' And I thought of how when I was younger, I might have been clumsier and more awkward than now, but instead I would have had something within me that could capture the heart of a girl like this. Here I was with a woman who was going through such terrible and unusual suffering and was struggling to face up to it and all I had done to help her was place caviar on crackers like an idiot and join her in washing it down with a little wine.

Mutsuko looked at me.

'Poor thing,' she said.

'Me?'

'You're reunited with your woman but she's becoming nothing more than a child. That kind of misfortune doesn't happen often.'

'I don't feel that way.'

'Do you like me better now than when I was in my twenties?'

'I like both.'

'See, I told you.'

'I'm not disappointed. In fact you may be at your most beautiful now. Did you have friends back then?'

'What do you mean by back then?'

'I mean, when you were this age. In the past.'

'To give you a simple answer, I could say I had many. But strictly speaking, I had none.'

'That's what I would have guessed. Anyone would feel a little hesitant in front of a girl as beautiful as this.'

'You don't have to be hesitant. I'm a sixty-seven-year-old grandmother. I'm like a ghost now.' And saying this, she stood up, surprisingly agile.

Then, nodding to my glass, she said, 'Don't spill it,' and proceeded to sit down on my lap.

'Am I heavy?'

'Not at all.'

And she wasn't at all. But her bottom was larger than I'd expected and I felt her body heat.

'You're just saying that,' she said, casually leaning back on me until I almost choked on her hair.

'Did you do this sort of thing with your father?'

'Of course not. I only did this kind of thing until I was seven or eight.'

'And now you're already a woman.'

'How does it feel, me sitting here now?'

'Like I've become a giant. Normally, I'd . . .'

'Normally?'

'Never mind.'

'What do you mean? Tell me how it feels normally?' And with that, she ground her hips into my crotch.

'Well, normally my thighs would start hurting before too long. Not that I've done this sort of thing for a long time.'

'Neither have I,' said Mutsuko. 'In fact, I've never done this kind of thing.'

'I'll put down my glass. I can't hold you properly like this.'

'I'll drink it for you.'

She tried to drink it all in one go. Unable to do so, she took a quick breath in between and accidentally spilled some from the corner of her mouth. I watched it trickle down her chin and onto her neck, then I licked it off her.

'You're still being somewhat hesitant,' she said. 'Are you afraid to touch my breasts?'

'I want to, but it's my hands that are hesitant.'

'Coward.'

She took my right hand and placed it against her breast.

'And the other one,' she followed, grabbing my left hand and placing it on her other breast.

'They're warm,' she said, taking a deep breath.

'I'm surprised. I didn't think they'd be this soft.'

'Well they wouldn't be hard, would they?'

'It's just that, considering the firmness of your skin, I thought they would be firmer too. But instead, they feel like cotton.'

'Maybe they do, but not for long.'

'I've . . . never touched a sixteen- or seventeen-year-old girl this way. Or in any way for that matter.'

'You see, now they're getting a little harder.'

Perhaps my touch tickled her as she leaned away from me slightly.

'You let a man get away with this and he might get carried away.'

'Get carried away then.'

'I want to take your clothes off.'

'So take them off.'

As I felt myself losing control, some words came to mind from R. P. Warren's novel *All the King's Men*: 'Can you figure out a single thing you really please-God like to do you can do and keep your dignity? The human frame just ain't built that way.'

'Photograph me,' said Mutsuko, naked.

'I don't have the camera with me.'

'Then photograph me tomorrow.'

'You won't leave, will you?'

'I won't leave.'

'You've said that before and left anyway.'

'I'm not going anywhere.'

'Let's take a shower.'

'Why? Do I smell of sweat?'

'Actually, it's myself I'm concerned about.'

'I don't mind.'

I frantically kissed her lips. And her neck and her breasts. It felt strange. Although it was a body I had already kissed every corner of, and done everything I could to, as I caressed her belly button and moved my hand down, I felt hesitant, as if I were committing a crime. My hand felt like something dirty and vulgar. I hesitantly reached down, past where her hair was still soft and thin, down to where I could feel the heat of her sex.

'It's so hot.'

'Yes.'

'So wet.'

'Don't feel you have to comment on everything.' She giggled.

'I wonder if it's all right for me to continue.'

'Why wouldn't it be?'

'You might be a virgin.'

'Then be the first.'

'But I wonder if it's all right for an over-the-hill middle-aged man to be doing this.'

'Then bring me a young man you think would be appropriate.'

'I don't want to do that.'

Mutsuko moved her hips.

'It's just that . . . seeing our naked bodies next to each other, I'm shocked by how unsightly I am.'

'Do you like saying that kind of thing?'

'Perhaps I'm a bit of a masochist.'

'Then I'll play along . . . Use your tongue. Move your fingers away and give me your tongue.'

And taking my time, savouring every moment, I took her virginity.

After we were done, Mutsuko became sentimental and she told me she wanted to hear some poetry.

'And how old is the Mutsuko that wants to hear it?'

'Sixty-seven . . . and sixteen . . . and seventeen.'

'Of course.'

'I can't choose one or the other.'

'I'm sorry, but I can't think of anything. It's not like that time before, when the words just came streaming out of my mouth.'

'That's because you were hospitalised back then. Now, once again, your mind is filled with the things of this world.'

'There's also the difficulty of having to satisfy two generations.'

'Not two generations. Just me.'

Words came forth from my mouth:

Me
You
'Us'
'We'
Cannot be reduced to me and you
That's why it's

Me
You
'Us'

'Why that poem?'
'I want to believe that we will survive, even if we are separated.'
'Who wrote it?'
'Taeko Tomioka.'
'I didn't know men read poetry by women.'
'Well, maybe I'm not normal.'
'Do you know it from when you were a student?'
'No. Which means I was reading this kind of thing even back when I had confidence in my abilities. Maybe that was one of the reasons why I didn't get promoted at work.'
'Is that the end? Even that by itself is beautiful.'
'It's not the end.'
I continued:

Me
You
Place our hands in each other's mouths
Touch our throats
Touch our windpipes
Touch our stomachs
Touch our lungs
Touch our hearts
Our diaphragms
Livers, pancreas, ribs, intestines
Muscles, arteries, veins, capillaries
We touch all kinds of things

All kinds of abstract names
What we can never touch
Is you
Is me

Mutsuko dozed off. I pulled the covers over her naked shoulders and felt like a father fixing the blankets of his child – even though I, only moments before, had been pushing myself inside her painfully thin body. I wondered to myself what would happen. What on earth would happen now?

6

There's a dusty road lined with shops in front of Ebisu station. It leads to a hilly residential area blending old houses with new concrete homes. Here and there it reminds you of twenty, thirty years ago, and you'd never think you were only a twelve- or thirteen-minute walk from Shibuya. In a forgotten corner of this area comprising old wooden homes, there was a dirty concrete apartment building. And in there was a small, two-bedroom apartment facing east on the second floor. That was the place that became our home.

Mutsuko still had the apartment she had been staying at before, but she said that she was 'keeping it for the next time I get that sluggish feeling again'. A middle-aged man can't say anything when a girl says that. As for me, I'd sent my company a letter requesting a leave of absence 'for a while, for personal reasons'. It was an incomprehensible letter, though I do say so myself, and I resigned myself to losing my job.

I couldn't say anything to my family. I went home to pick up the camera and a few belongings. I thought about leaving a note but left the house without doing so. It would have been different if I were going to write the truth, but I felt that anything other than the truth would simply be an attempt to leave open the possibility of returning. I probably had two months with Mutsuko at the most, at which point her 'sluggishness' would return and I would be left alone. I didn't want to keep the possibility of returning to my job and my family in anticipation of that day. I felt like I'd somehow be betraying Mutsuko if I did that.

I knew I shouldn't have left home without even leaving a simple note saying 'Don't worry' or 'Don't look for me'. But, selfishly, I figured that Mutsuko was much more alone than my wife at that moment, and I didn't want to betray her – not even behind her back. 'We're okay for money,' Mutsuko had said. 'There's enough for two years, even if we live a little luxuriously. I probably can't live that long, so don't worry about it. All you have to do is keep me in your arms.'

We spent our entire days naked. At times we'd turn the air conditioner to really cold, then rub each other warm once we felt like we were freezing. Other times we turned the air conditioner off and opened the window on the side where people couldn't look in. But there was no breeze from the window and we both got covered in sweat. So we pressed our bodies together, rubbing our sweat against each other.

Everything we did was accompanied by the thought that this wouldn't last. And although I didn't want to think that worked as a stimulus, it was true that our passion was intensified by our desire to make the maximum use of limited time. My sexual prowess didn't let me down – though this may have been due to some mysterious and whimsical power endowed upon me. In fact, I could come over and over again in the same day and still want Mutsuko just as badly the next.

'It's just the way you can be, if you don't have any worries on your mind.' Mutsuko said between breaths, while we were in the heat of the moment. 'Even forty-eight-year-olds – have –

strength. Thinking – about – the next day – and being bound by – responsibilities – and obligations – makes them weak – Yes!'

'Let's keep it down a little.'

'I just forget.'

'Should we go ahead and buy that potted morning glory we saw on the way back from the baths?'

'Buy a darkroom.'

'A darkroom?'

'You said – that there was – a DIY darkroom.'

'We can develop the pictures – without going to all that trouble.'

'Then, you do it – the way you want.'

'All right.'

'In the afternoon – let's go – buy it.'

'All right.'

'What kinds of things – do you need?'

'Measuring cup – stirring stick – funnel – timer – thermometer – developing tank – sponge – tongs.'

* * *

Mutsuko naked and in her twenties, and Mutsuko naked as a sixteen-, seventeen-year-old; her smile, her sex, all appear as negatives in the developer. White pubic hair on a black naked body. Mutsuko with white hair and black teeth. I hung the rolls of film up, wiped them off with a sponge and hung weighted clips on them as they dried. We opened the window and lay down on the bed together.

'Oh no,' said Mutsuko. 'There isn't a single photo of you.'

'It can't be helped. I was the photographer.'

'I can't believe that I didn't once think to photograph you.'

'That's how it is.'

'How what is?'

'Well, everyone has that side to them.'

'Why didn't you say something? Why didn't you say, "Take a picture of me"?'

'I was happy taking photos of you.'

'Were you going to tell me afterwards? That I'm always thinking about myself?'

'I wasn't thinking that.'

'I'm going to photograph you.'

'You don't need to.'

'Well I'm going to. Get naked.'

'It will only be grotesque.'

'If you won't do it, I'll take your clothes off myself.'

We joked around in a way that I would have normally found silly or tiresome. But there, with her, I wasn't getting fed up of it at all.

In the photographs from her twenties, Mutsuko's breasts were much larger, her body more voluptuous, and I hesitated in complimenting them.

'I'm all skin and bones now, aren't I?' she said.

'No, that's not true. Your backside is surprisingly soft and large.'

'But my breasts now, compared to those then.'

'Don't you worry; a dirty-minded middle-aged man like me finds your body even more stimulating now.'

'But I've become so young,' she lamented, rubbing her breasts and arms. Unable to find any words to console her, I held her to me.

'What do you want me to do?' I said. 'I want to do whatever

you want, but I don't know what to do.'

'Take my nipples in your mouth.'

'All right.'

'Just like nobody can console a person who is getting old – a person who is getting closer and closer to death – nobody can console me as I get younger and disappear. It's not your fault. This nipple next.'

'All right.'

'This is all you have to do. If I wasn't sixty-seven, I might not have been able to stand this cruel twist of fate. But being the old person that I am, I'm able to enjoy this transformation. I even want to thank this freak of nature for letting me experience such happiness before I die. All you have to do is be here. Just by doing that, you are already sacrificing many things, like your company and family. I've been acting like I haven't been taking notice, but I've been so grateful. Now it's my turn. This time I'm going to eat you up. Let me go. Now you lie down. Oh, you've gone all limp, poor thing. You're thinking about my future too, are you? It's okay. Don't worry about it. Become big inside me. Inside my mouth.'

And there, amid the photographs of Mutsuko in her twenties, the sixteen-, seventeen-year-old Mutsuko and I lost track of time and revelled in being as obscene as we pleased.

On the tenth night, Mutsuko came running back home. I got a terrible sense of foreboding as I heard her footsteps rushing up the stairs outside the apartment, and my hands – which were about to slice a cucumber – stopped moving. I could feel her fumbling to unlock the door, so I ran over, unlocked it and opened it. Mutsuko looked up at me surprised. Her face was pale.

'What happened?'

'They were out of tofu.'

'Something happened, didn't it?'

She nodded.

'What happened?'

'Something unpleasant.'

'What was it?'

Mutsuko slipped off her sandals, walked past me towards the window and looked down. I quickly shut the door and locked it, then went over next to her and looked down out of the window. Through the screen I could see the street lamps on the narrow asphalt road. The shutters of the old shop across the way were down as always. And painted on the grey shutters in peeling black paint were the words 'Interior decoration – wallpaper, carpets, chair covers'. There was nobody on the street.

'The police,' said Mutsuko, closing the window and turning the air conditioning on.

'They were on patrol?'

She nodded. 'Two of them.'

'What did they want?'

'They asked what year I was born.'

'Knowing that you live here?'

'Yes. I told them I just graduated. That way it won't be a problem that I'm not in school.'

'Right.'

'"Did you really?" they said. They said I looked like I was still a schoolgirl.'

'Well, it's none of their business.'

'Then they asked me who I live with. I told them you were my uncle. But they kept asking me if you were really a relative. I asked them why they would think otherwise, but instead of answering they just asked me where my home was. And what my father's name was. And what the name of the school I graduated from was. The two of them asked me one question after the other. I told them I hadn't done anything wrong and tried to run away, but one of them grabbed me by the arm and said, "We're not saying you did anything wrong. We got a phone call from someone and we're just worried. Are you sure you're not being forced to stay with your uncle?"'

'It's the guy next door,' I said.

'I told them I wasn't being forced to do anything and that there was nothing to be worried about and shrugged them off.'

'That young guy,' I continued, 'he must have been listening in on us. I got that feeling when I bumped into him in the hallway two, three days ago. I can understand if a single guy like him listens in, but he didn't need to call the police.'

'But it's true that I only look like I'm in school, so if a girl that age was living with you and having sex with you, I can understand why he might worry that it's a kidnapping.'

'I think we're both getting the picture.'

'We are. What should we do?'

'What do you mean, "What should we do?"'

'Well, they might question you next.'

'I'll brush them off,' I told her.

'The police might decide to take the minor into their custody,' she countered.

'I'll make them go away.'

'That'll only make them more suspicious.'

'But what kind of explanation can I give them?' I asked her. 'The person who called the police knows we're not family.

Knows that we're having sex. And that you are the age you are.'

'I'll find something to tell them.'

'What? That you're actually sixty-seven?'

'Of course not.'

'Well, what other explanation could you give them? We can't tell them your place of birth, the name of your parents, or your school. All we can do is lie. They'll see through the lies easily. You'll be taken into custody, we'll be separated and precious time will be wasted.'

'That doesn't mean we can get away with not opening the door and just telling them to go away,' she said.

'They might not come anyway,' I replied.

'But they might.'

'What's most important is that *you're* free. You should go to your other apartment; the one I don't know the location of.'

'We can look for another apartment together.'

'Okay. Let's do that. At any rate, let's pack up our things so we're ready to leave at any time.'

'I don't want people to see the photographs,' she added.

'Okay.'

'I can't believe that we're getting disturbed like this,' I moaned to myself.

'Someone's coming up.'

'What?'

'I hear footsteps coming up the stairs,' she hissed. 'There are two of them. It must be the police.'

'You don't have the pistol on you, do you?'

'It's at the other apartment.'

'Not that we could use it, even if it were here.'

I could hear the footsteps coming down the hallway.

'You get out of here. I don't want you to waste your precious time with this.'

'But I don't want to leave you.'

There was a loud knock on the door.

'Here. These are the negatives and photographs. I want to keep them, but if I have to go to the police, they might see them.'

'But I don't want to leave you.'

Another knock. The cops called out a name in a low, calm voice. The false name we used to rent this place.

'We're from the local police box.'

'I'm coming,' I said.

Mutsuko stuffed the negatives and photographs into a big plastic bag. There was another knock on the door. I looked at Mutsuko and she looked back at me. Then I unlocked the door and opened it a crack. There was a plump cop in uniform who looked to be in his forties. Behind him was a tall cop who looked like he might even be in his early twenties. Both of them were looking at me with no emotion on their faces.

'Is there something I can do for you?'

'We're sorry for bothering you so late at night,' said the one in his forties. The one in his twenties immediately echoed, 'We're sorry,' probably just as he was taught.

'Could we talk to you for a moment?' the older cop continued.

'What's this about?'

'Would you mind if we came in and talked?'

'Sure, come in,' I said, stepping back. Then I turned to Mutsuko and said, 'Say hello to your mother for me, then.' I turned back to the older cop and said, 'She's my niece. She's running an errand for me.'

The cop didn't respond. He just looked like he was wondering how to handle the situation.

'Excuse me,' said Mutsuko, carrying the large plastic bag over her shoulder. Then, as she was about to put on her sandals, the older cop asked, 'Going to your mother's?'

'Yes, I am,' she replied, as if wondering why anyone would question such a thing. Then she put on her sandals. 'Excuse me.'

'Can you hold on for just a little while?' said the older cop.

'What could you want with her?' I said.

'Where is your mother?'

'In Nakano.'

'Where in Nakano?'

'You can go,' I said, interrupting him. 'They don't have the right to ask such questions.'

'I'm sorry, but I think we'd better take you to Nakano ourselves,' said the older cop.

'Go back inside,' said the younger cop as he guided her back into the room by her shoulders. Mutsuko shrugged him off.

'What's going on?' I asked.

'I don't know; there's something about this room that isn't normal,' said the older cop, suddenly getting on his high horse.

'If that's what you think, I'll listen to what you have to say. But leave the girl out of this.'

'You keep saying girl. Are you treating her like one? A young girl?'

'What are you trying to say?'

'That's equipment for developing photos, isn't it?'

'Yes.'

'And there's nothing else in the room.'

'Everything else is in the closet.'

'The kitchen utensils too?'

'I mostly eat out. This is all I need.'

The cop turned to Mutsuko. 'Sweetheart,' he said. 'Did this man take photographs of you?'

'I did,' I cut in. 'Is that a crime?'

'If you were taking normal photos, would you get this kind of equipment to develop them?' said the older cop, high-handed again as he fixed me with a glare.

'There are plenty of people who develop photographs themselves.'

'We've been informed.'

'About what?'

'That you two aren't normal.'

'Do we have to be normal?'

'I don't want to have to say this in front of her.'

'Then let her leave.'

'I suppose you're planning to meet up with her somewhere later.'

'I don't know what you're talking about.'

'I'm leaving,' said Mutsuko. 'I'm going to be late.'

Mutsuko pushed passed the young cop. 'Bye.'

'Hey, wait a second,' called out the younger cop, before turning to the older one and asking, 'Should I go after her?'

Behind him I could hear Mutsuko running down the stairs in her sandals.

'No, it's okay,' said the older cop. 'There's nothing we can do. Leave it.'

'I'm sorry,' said the younger cop.

'Okay, you're sorry, I just can't count on you, can I?'

'If she's a suspect, then we–'

'We don't know that, do we?'

'No, sir.'

'To be frank,' said the older cop, turning back to me again, 'we've been told that you and that girl are at it.'

'At what?'

'You know.'

'No, I'm afraid I don't know.'

'Come on, there's only one thing I could be hinting at here. How old is she, anyway? She said she just graduated from school, but it's hard to believe.'

'Are you questioning what she said?'

'The guarantor of the lease,' said the older cop. 'When you rented this room. It's made up, isn't it? We checked and there was no such person at the address. This is a crime, you know.'

'I suppose if I cause trouble it would be.'

'Even if she has graduated from school, that still only makes her seventeen or eighteen. What are you doing with a girl like that?'

'Her parents have separated. I'm just looking after her for the moment.'

'In a room like this? Without working?'

'I'm out of work at present. I want to get a better room, but I don't have the money for it.'

'But you can afford to buy brand-new developing equipment, I see.'

'It was a gift.'

'Okay. Can you come to the station with us?'

'But she'll be coming back and she doesn't have a key.'

'It'll take her at least an hour to get to Nakano and back. We'll be done before then.'

I couldn't possibly go. A girl named Mutsuko didn't even exist. There was no way I would be able to answer their questions. I needed to escape. But what could I possibly do against these two men? If that fickle, unknown power helped revive my kendo sword-fighting abilities back to my peak level, I might have been able to put up a fight. But I didn't get the feeling that that kind of miracle was about to happen.

'Let's go,' said the older cop.

There was nothing else I could do. I realised I'd been in a sleeveless undershirt all this time, so I grabbed an open-collar shirt hanging from the wall. I put it on as well as a pair of socks, my mind racing with thoughts of escape. It would have helped if I had trainers. But all I had were sandals and black work shoes. I could run faster in the shoes, so I decided to wear those. I closed and locked the windows.

Whatever happened, I thought to myself, it had been a wonderful ten days. And at the back of my mind, I'd had the feeling that all of this had been too good to be true, so now I felt it couldn't be helped if I was to be thrown in jail. Immediately I brushed that thought aside. After all, if I let that happen, Mutsuko would be left all alone. Then, sooner or later, she'd be seized by another wave of youth – one that would make it even more difficult for her to live. I knew I had to be able to move around freely. I knew I couldn't abandon her.

'You look ready to me,' said the older cop, hurrying me.

Both of them stepped out into the hall and I put on my shoes. I looked back at the room. There was no way to escape. I turned off the lights, stepped out into the hall, then closed and locked the door behind me.

The older cop walked down the stairs in front of me, while

the young cop followed behind. As the three of us clattered down the iron stairs I wondered if the person who'd called the police was quietly watching me being led away. As we were reaching the bottom of the stairs, a black shadow suddenly jumped out from underneath them and the older cop let out a startled shout.

'I'm sorry.'

It was Mutsuko.

'What is it?' What was she doing?

'I'd accidentally taken your wallet with me,' she said, handing me a fat wallet.

'It's okay.'

'It's not.'

'But you'll need it.'

'I have enough. I'm okay.'

Her eyes told me to hurry up and take it.

'If you don't hurry, it'll be late by the time you get back,' I said.

'Yes.'

Mutsuko watched me take the wallet and put it in my pocket. Then she said, 'This too,' and brought out her left hand from behind her back. It was a long stick that looked like the handle of a mop. I felt a burst of excitement in the back of my head.

'What's that?'

The older cop tried to reach for it, but I was quicker. In one motion I took the stick from her and tackled the young cop behind me. The older cop jumped back and tried to reach for his pistol, but I struck him on the shoulder hard and fast. I turned round to see the young cop, still sprawled against the stairs, reaching for his gun. I struck him on the arm, then flipped round and struck the older cop's arm. Strangely, nobody cried out.

'Let's go!' shouted Mutsuko, and she ran out into the street.

I followed right behind her, passing through the narrow space next to the apartment, through the gate and out onto the street. Her young back, running as fast as she could towards Shibuya. I followed through the empty night-time residential streets where there was nobody around to get in our way.

I couldn't possibly have this much stamina, I thought to myself. Somebody was endowing me with strength again. And if that was the case, then I should be okay, should be able to run as far as I needed to. My body felt like that of a different person. A body different from the one that had got out of breath running away from the cinema. A different body from the one that couldn't even help Mutsuko. Now I felt I could even carry her on my back if I wanted. Though I didn't want to imagine what people would make of a man running with a girl on his back at this time of night. I was calm. I just wanted to find some place as soon as possible where Mutsuko and I could catch our breath and laugh about all this together. I wanted to compliment her on her quick thinking.

Mutsuko was fast. I was surprised she could run so well. Maybe she'd been endowed with supernatural powers, too. As long as we were together there was nothing to be afraid of. Nothing. Mutsuko.

'Mutsuko!' I called out in a small voice to her back, but she was as fast as the wind.

'Mutsuko!'

The wide uphill street became a narrow, gentle downhill street, and we eventually came out onto a wide street again.

That's when I lost sight of her. I was quite certain that she had turned left on the wide street, but once I reached the road she was nowhere to be seen. Surely it wasn't possible to lose sight of her on such a wide street in a residential area empty of cars. I turned round and looked up the street we'd just come down, but there was no sign of her following. Standing still, leaning against the corner wall, I called her name out quietly.

'Mutsuko.'

I couldn't help but smile. It was a joke. As soon as I'd said her name, she popped out from behind one of the houses, smiling.

'You naughty girl.'

I was about to take a step towards her. But a look of surprise suddenly flashed across her face. She'd seen something behind me. I turned round and was bathed in bright light. Headlights coming closer and closer.

'Don't move,' boomed a voice through a loudspeaker.

'Run!' I shouted.

'No.' She shook her head firmly.

'Just go!'

She took a few steps back.

'Hurry!'

She began to run.

'Don't move.'

This time the voice wasn't from a loudspeaker. It was right behind me. Resigned, I put up my arms, though I may have been able to escape if I'd tried.

'Put down the stick.'

Remembering only then that I was still holding it, I threw it on the ground in front of me. A man's hand grabbed my right wrist, pulled it down and cuffed it. And for some reason, I felt a sense of conclusion, of finality. As if I'd been secretly hoping this would happen all along.

7

A single fallen leaf sat on top of the table. It was mid November. The table was outside, between two buildings, and a small ray of light had found its way through the high-rises, the trees, the poles and other obstacles to shine down on its surface. The different colours of the leaf – the deep yellow-brown of the narrow, oval tip, the vivid yellow in the middle and the little bit of green that remained at the stem – were all sparkling in the late-autumn morning sun. This ragged-edged leaf also had a couple of insect holes, and I admired it as I sat with my paper cup of self-serve coffee in front of me.

On the night of the incident, I'd been arrested and detained at Shibuya police station. The questioning had begun the next day, and I'd immediately admitted to resisting arrest and assaulting the police officers. However, I'd refused to give them my name or to tell them anything about Mutsuko.

I was certain that the police couldn't do anything about Mutsuko as long as I didn't say anything about her. In fact, by the end of the second day, they'd already stopped asking about her and the questioning began to focus instead on the thinking behind the assault. Again they told me to tell them my name.

'Obstruction of justice is a serious crime, you know.'

They told me that both policemen had suffered injuries that would take ten days to heal, though that told me nothing about how seriously they had been injured.

After two days, my ten-day detention period began, which was later extended by another ten days. They'd shouted at me, saying this was a minor offence. That I wouldn't be prosecuted for it if I told them the truth. But that I would be tried if I continued to be so stubborn – which would leave a permanent mark on my record.

On the twelfth day I finally told them my name and address. They contacted my wife, and apparently she'd come to Shibuya police station. I only guessed this as the elderly prosecutor started saying things to me like, 'A deputy director at a first-rate construction company coming to this . . .' and, 'The numbers seem to be on the rise these days. People promoted to managerial positions, then just falling apart.'

Soon enough, the topic of Mutsuko was brought up again. I told them that I didn't know anything about her, and that I absolutely did not have any sexual relations with her. I refused to budge on those points.

'Well, I'm afraid if you persist in sticking to that story, we have no other option than to prosecute you.'

In mid August I was transferred to the Tokyo Detention Centre. And as the secure vehicle carrying me made its way through the city, I pressed my face to its screened windows, scanning the streets for a sign of Mutsuko.

On the second day at the detention centre I saw my wife. She couldn't look me in the eyes and simply said something to the effect that I would be able to get out if we posted bail, but because bail was set at 1.5 million yen it would take some time.

'Don't worry about bail,' I told her. 'There's no need to waste that kind of money on me.'

'I can't do that, can I?' She looked up at the ceiling, annoyed.

'I've caused you enough trouble already. I've been selfish. I think it would serve me right to have to stay here. There's no need to spend 1.5 million yen. Tell them I refused bail.'

'You say that, but—'

'Just tell them I've gone mad. That I'm being stubborn.'

'Do you think I can go around telling people that?'

She left the bento box she'd bought at the prison kiosk and went home. She didn't post the bail, though, so I spent my time sharing a cell with some sort of robber who claimed he was in there due to simple bad luck and who bored me with his endless complaints.

After a while the government appointed a lawyer to represent me; he told me that I'd be tried for resisting arrest and obstruction of justice. Twenty-three days after I'd been detained, my trial took place. And on that same day a verdict was handed down.

My wife had taken the stand as a character witness and she'd told the court how I had been a hard worker until I had been appointed deputy director. And how I'd had a mental breakdown since moving to the Northern Japan branch on my own. She went on to explain that I'd remained a kind-hearted husband throughout all of this and to say that if I were to be released with a suspended sentence, she would make it her personal responsibility to take the utmost care of me to ensure I didn't offend again. I felt that everyone had sealed off their emotions. As if we were all playing a game of not being human.

After an hour and a half, the guilty verdict was given and sentence was passed – a six-month custodial sentence to be suspended for two years. I went home with my wife in a taxi, and as soon as I got in the cab she said, 'You've gained weight.'

When we got home, my son opened the front door and said, 'You're home,' without even looking at me, then went straight upstairs.

Once seated on the living-room couch, I asked about my company. My wife told me that they'd been kind enough to treat my situation as if I'd been requested to hand in my resignation, so they would pay me my full retirement allowance. She told me several names of people at the company who I'd thought I'd lost all connection with and how they'd gone out of their way to make sure I was looked after. And for the first time through everything, tears welled up in my eyes. As for my wife, her tone remained unfailingly harsh.

'I'm going to leave it at that for now,' she said, 'because I don't want to bombard you with one thing after the other.'

'It's okay. Say whatever you need to. It'll only bother me if things are left unsaid.'

'After what I said in court, I will have to wait two years before doing the paperwork. But once that's passed, I'm planning to leave you.'

'I understand.' I thought that it was only natural.

The next day, my son still wasn't talking to me. In fact, I sensed he might even be afraid of me. It was as if he couldn't get used to the idea that this man who had been arrested and found guilty in court was his father.

From the morning of my third day back at home, I began leaving the house, saying, 'I'm going to look for a job.' Neither my wife nor son responded at all.

I walked through Shinjuku, Shibuya and Ebisu in search of Mutsuko. And when I couldn't find her after a week of searching, I started spending most of my time in the outdoor café in the high-rise in Shinjuku where I'd taken pictures of her not so long ago. My walking around had done no good, so I thought that I ought to stay in one place and see if she might come to me.

So there I was in mid November, sitting staring at a fallen leaf. Assuming that Mutsuko started feeling 'sluggish' around the end of August and she had woken up to find herself younger again at the end of September, that would make her now . . . what? Ten? Six? . . . Two? If the length of time she had at one age was about one month now, I wondered if she might even have gone through a second transformation at the end of October; in which case, perhaps she wasn't even any longer on this earth.

I tried to console myself – telling myself that there was no way I should assume that her body was sticking to any kind of pattern. After all, it was possible that she could just show up suddenly, looking just the way she did before – in a sweater and coat and with a big smile on her face. Exactly like the girl who had just walked past me down the path to the station. It was possible that she could appear in front of me as a woman in her twenties, as a girl of seventeen or eighteen, or as a woman in her forties. She could even have returned to being a sixty-seven-year-old.

The fallen leaves that day were beautiful. They reminded me of the film *Portrait of Jennie*, starring Jennifer Jones, and that reminded me of Mutsuko. I was amazed I hadn't seen that connection earlier. It was a story of a young girl who appears in front of a poor painter one day and grows into a beautiful woman in a short time. Then she is swept away by a wave one stormy night. It was a tale of how a young girl becomes a woman – an experience every woman goes through – and of a death that came long before its time. The speed at which time passed in the story was very similar to Mutsuko's situation. There seemed to be something special about Jennie's existence, and the poor painter who meets her was supposed to be just the rare and kind-hearted kind of man who could see that.

But what could people take from my Mutsuko? What could anybody possibly be able to take from my incomprehensible existence? If I had indeed been chosen by God to experience this, then surely he'd chosen me while drunk and blindfolded. I didn't have the right or worthiness to challenge socially accepted values. All I'd done was to selfishly lose myself in an affair, take risqué pictures and to go down on a girl even though she was only sixteen or seventeen. It had never occurred to me to paint a single portrait. You could, of course, argue that I didn't paint her because I wasn't a painter. But when you think of the photographs I took instead, they were driven only by desire and never for a moment by aesthetics. All in all, my reaction to this . . . this miracle had been nothing short of pathetic. I'd derived no revelation from it. All I'd done was felt desire for Mutsuko, become useless, then ended up staring at a dead leaf on a table.

But I wasn't getting bored with staring at this leaf at all. Quite the contrary, it was as if it was the first time in a very long time that I'd taken a moment to enjoy a season. I'd experienced the northern Japanese winter, the spring before cherry blossoms, and a hot, humid summer with Mutsuko. But with my mind always occupied with other thoughts, I'd never been able to appreciate the seasons.

I gently moved my hand along the table towards the leaf. I touched the yellow of it with the tip of my finger and it made me want to embrace its beauty. But I couldn't. It would be impossible. It being so small and fragile, there was no way I could impose myself upon it. Immediately I knew what I was really afraid of. I was worried that Mutsuko might have regressed to a sperm and an egg. Which of the two would her soul remain in? And was she about to disappear for ever? I got the feeling that this was indeed what had happened to her.

No. No, I couldn't let that happen. I pinned the leaf down with the tip of my fingers to keep it from escaping. I watched it wriggle and squirm in the morning sun, but I didn't let it go. As it moved, I stroked it with the fingertips of my other hand as if to soothe it. And as I did so, tears welled up in my eyes. I had such a strong feeling that Mutsuko was somewhere facing death right at that very moment and that there was nothing I could do about it. It was a feeling that crushed me and made tears trickle down my cheeks. Then I felt as if I was being watched. I looked up, my eyes all a blur. And there, standing a few paces from me, was a small girl.

I watched her, unable to move for a while. As if time itself had stopped. It was Mutsuko. I guessed she was about four or five years old. She was wearing a dark brown dress with frills on the shoulders and she was looking right at me. Her white skin, her eyes, her mouth, nose, ears – everything about her was small, cute, doll-like and fragile, I felt that she might break at the slightest touch. Her eyes were filled with tears.

'I didn't know how you were,' she said in a child's voice, but with a tone that was unmistakably the adult Mutsuko.

'I know.'

She came closer. I couldn't stand up.

'This age is a real inconvenience. It's hard to walk the streets alone, let alone go shopping. Whatever I try to do, somebody gets in the way. Coming here was really difficult, too.'

The small girl flashed a cheeky smile at me with tears still in her eyes.

'There'll be good things about it, too,' I said, gazing at her. 'For instance, if I pick you up now and nestle your cheek against mine, nobody will suspect a thing.'

'That's true.' She nodded, wiping away her tears with cute, tiny hands. Then she smiled at me: 'Daddy.' And I swept her up in my arms.

She was so small and soft, I had to be gentle not to hurt her. I was struck by how terrifyingly light she was. She pushed her lips strongly against my cheek and I felt the clean and generous saliva of a small child. I placed my lips on her cheek as well and drew her face to mine.

'Ouch.'

'What?'

'Your beard.'

Even though I knew that she was the adult Mutsuko trapped in a child's body, I almost couldn't help myself saying, 'Oh, I'm sorry,' as if I was talking to a child. 'It's all right,' I said instead. 'Everything is going to be all right now I'm with you. I'll carry you anywhere you want. We can buy whatever you want. And we can eat whatever you want.'

Mutsuko sat on my lap and put her arms around my neck. 'I want to buy some clothes,' she said. 'These are dirty.'

'Then let's go to the department store. Hey we could . . . no, that's funny.'

'What is?'

'I was going to suggest we go on the amusement ride on the roof.'

Mutsuko laughed and, as she did, tears flowed from her eyes. She put her head against my cheek and cried. I stroked her hair and gently patted her on the back as I walked towards the store.

I was glad. Glad I was able to see her again. I felt as if I were walking on air and I thought of the ridiculous notions that had gone through my mind. Sperm and egg? How could I have been so dumb?

As I carried her, she never felt any heavier and I never got tired. And as I felt the warmth of her body, I was filled with happiness.

'How did you manage to buy these clothes on your own?'

'Well, did you notice how they're too big?'

'Are they?'

'Yes, they're a little big on me.'

'Well, they look really nice on you.'

'I bought a few outfits towards the end of my previous age.'

'That was smart of you.'

'Clothes for seven- to eight-year-olds, for five- to six-year-olds and three- to four-year-olds. These are for five- to six-year-olds and they're a little big.'

'And how about food?'

'I carry a shopping list and cash in hand, so I can pretend I'm running an errand for my mother.'

'I see.'

'People begin to notice you when you go many times. So I went to different shops all over the place and somehow managed to get by.'

'How about the apartment? Don't your neighbours notice that you're there all alone?'

'That's not a problem. I chose a place where people don't notice. I chose it when I was in my twenties with that in mind. That's not a problem, but–'

'But?'

'It's a lot of trouble to go to the bank to pay the rent.'

'I would imagine so.'

'I thought about it a lot, and I was finally able to do it by taking three months' rent with me together with a letter and explaining that my mother was sick.'

'I see.'

'The most difficult thing is walking through large, crowded areas, like Shinjuku and Shibuya. Those aren't the kind of places where four-year-olds usually walk around on their own. People always ask me questions when I'm on trains as well. Even when I thought you might show up at a certain place, I couldn't stay in one place for too long without looking suspicious.'

A woman walking past looked at us, surprised. It must have been because of Mutsuko's adult-like eloquence.

'You should probably talk a little more like a child when other people can hear you,' I said quietly.

'Daddy, you've lost weight.'

'Yeah, I'm afraid I have. I gained a little for a while, but I lost a lot while I was looking for you. You're managing so well, Mutsuko. You're a good girl. A good . . . look how small you've become.'

'Don't cry.'

'No, I won't. Don't worry, Daddy isn't crying.'

At the department store, father and daughter bought clothes, including an overcoat, socks, shoes and a small shoulder bag. Then we chose a restaurant and had an early lunch. It was only a little past eleven and the restaurant was almost empty. The daughter became full after eating just one piece of fried shrimp and seeing this brought tears to her father's eyes once again.

'I want to stay at a hotel,' said my cheeky daughter.

A plump lady sitting across from us heard her, smiled and said to me, 'What a cute thing to say.'

I smiled back, then leaned in to Mutsuko and whispered, 'Can't we go to your apartment instead?'

'No, we can't.'

'Why not?'

'I want a hotel.'

'Don't trouble your father like that, darling,' interrupted the plump lady.

Once we left the restaurant, with me carrying Mutsuko in my arms, she said she was sleepy.

'It's partially because I'm relieved to see you, but I also just don't have much energy,' she said.

'You should sleep. I'll be like a mobile bed for you.'

'Will you reserve a hotel room?'

'Why can't we go to your apartment?'

'We can't.'

'Why not?'

'You, me, us, remember?'

'Fine. I'll take you to the hotel while you're sleeping.'

Trusting everything to me, Mutsuko closed her eyes. As we left the department store, I whispered a question that had been on my mind, though it wouldn't have bothered me if she was already asleep.

'How long has it been? Since you've become like this, I mean.'

With her cheek still against my shoulder, she responded

sleepily, 'A little over two months.'

A shudder swept through my body. Surely that meant that she didn't have much time left. No, if I went by the way things had happened before, then she should have experienced the transformation already. Mutsuko suddenly felt heavier in my arms, meaning that she must have fallen asleep. Could this mean that this was as young as she was going to get? That maybe she might start to grow older again? These were things I'd considered before and now such thoughts were flooding back into my mind. Could it be that Mutsuko had been waiting for me – just like the way a sick person on their deathbed stays alive, barely breathing, until the people they care for arrive? Could it be that Mutsuko, with her small body, had been hanging on until the day she could see me again? If that were the case, then it was no surprise that she'd fallen asleep from exhaustion. She should sleep. Sleep in peace. But the truth was I wanted her to wake up as soon as possible. There were so many things I wanted to talk to her about. So many things I wanted to ask.

The hotel room we got was on the twenty-fifth floor. Unlike the views at the other rooms we'd stayed at, from this one you could see a baseball field and an elevated road against a background of several skyscrapers.

I gently laid Mutsuko down on the bed. How small she was. To think that she'd made a transfer at the bank, gone shopping for food and lived alone with these cute little feet, those tiny hands and that little body, made me want to hold her tight, and I stood there looking down at her for a while, trying to resist the temptation to do so. I placed a blanket over her, then got down on my knees. I couldn't take my eyes off this girl's beautiful sleeping face.

Twenty minutes later Mutsuko opened her eyes with barely any warning. They looked at me straight away, but at first they were like glass balls. Light gradually returned to them, then she smiled at me. I smiled back and nodded.

'I'm embarrassed,' she said.

'Don't be. I'm glad you got some sleep.'

'What floor are we on?'

'The twenty-fifth.'

'Just like the room we stayed in before.'

'Yes, although the view is in a slightly different direction.'

'You're right.'

When she sat up, the bed looked even bigger.

'I'm surprised,' I said.

'About what?'

'How pretty you were at every stage of your life.'

'It feels like I'm looking at old photographs,' she smiled. 'I'd forgotten I looked like this myself.'

She sounded like a very precocious girl talking confidently like an adult. But I found it intoxicating.

'Will you draw me a bath?'

'Of course,' I replied and walked to the bathroom and began to fill it up.

While it was running, I stuck my head out into the bedroom and saw Mutsuko standing by the large window looking out. She was small. A beautiful, extraordinary creature, and I felt something like pity constrict my chest. I think she sensed I was watching her and I saw her draw in a breath to speak.

'I'm sorry . . . so sorry,' she said, 'but please understand . . . I have to go.'

My mind went blank for a moment, as if suffering concussion.

'Where?' I said.

'I have no time.'

'I'll follow you anywhere.'

'Don't be so difficult.'

'I'm not being difficult.'

'I don't have the strength to hit you and leave you like before.'

'Why would you leave me?'

'I want to. I need to. You and I, we can't sleep with the same dreams. This is the same. It's something I have to do alone.'

'But what's going to happen now?'

'I don't know, but it's probably what you are expecting.'

'It might not be.'

'I know it will. I was praying to God. To wait until I could see you again. Even if just for a moment. Now I've run out of strength. I'm feeling it again.'

'No. I don't want to leave you alone.'

'Don't do this, please. Let me go quietly.'

'Will we meet again?'

'I'm sure.'

'But where?'

'I don't know. This is the first time for me to experience this, too. I'm afraid of what's going to happen.'

'Then let's go through it together.'

'No. The one thing I know is that I can't take you with me. Just like I don't know what will happen to me after I die. But I do know that I *will* die.'

'I don't want to hear you make connections like that.'

'Look, I have to go. Don't say anything more.'

'But I want to spend at least one night with you.'

'I said I'd be satisfied if I could see you for just one moment.

This time together was more than I asked for.'

'Why tie yourself down like that?'

'I have to. Because if I don't, I know something irrevocable will happen.'

'What kind of thing?'

'I told you, I don't know! I don't know, but I feel it.'

'I don't want to be separated from you for ever.'

'Please let me go. I have to go.'

She looked at me with determination in her eyes. And though I could have protested more, I accepted her wishes.

Our relationship had been one based on miracles. One in which I'd been made to feel my own powerlessness. I'd known we were dealing with destiny. Dealing with something that couldn't be controlled by people. That's how I felt. Or was it merely how I was being made to feel? It seemed the only thing I could do was to make peace with and accept this. And as these thoughts went through my mind, I could feel my body being drained of all strength and going limp, like a marionette released from the hands of a puppeteer.

I got down on my knees and a cry escaped my lips. It sounded like a sob, but tears didn't fall from my eyes. I was too crushed to even cry properly. I didn't want to lose her. Seeing me like this, she came to me and placed her small hand on my bowed head.

* * *

As the autumn sunlight drew long shadows and bathed the city in late-evening colours, I held Mutsuko in my arms. As if we were father and daughter, we walked out of the hotel, along the walkway and towards the street.

'Let me down,' she said.

And I should have done so. That had been our promise, after all. But instead I carried her all the way down to the street where people were passing by.

'Let me down here,' she said.

'Why do you want to leave so soon?' I moaned quietly, unable to help myself.

'Goodbye,' she whispered in my ear and I could tell she was holding back tears.

'Yeah,' I replied, but I couldn't bring myself to put her down. I saw people walking by us and when I looked up I saw the yellow-brown leaves on the trees moving gently in the wind against a sky bathed in evening sun. Some of the leaves were falling and I heard her whisper again.

'Goodbye,' she said.

I nodded and let her down onto the pavement. Then I forced myself to smile.

'Goodbye,' I breathed.

Mutsuko looked up at me and nodded with tearful eyes. Then she turned and began walking towards the station. I watched her, helpless and alone as she moved through the crowd, the line between her and me broken by strangers walking in between. Her light pink dress wound its way between large suits and women. Then eventually, she disappeared.